TIMMER

3 50

WB

JUDGE DEE AT WORK

These eight stories, featuring the master-detective of Ancient China and his assistants Ma Joong, Sergeant Hoong and Chiao Tai, cover a decade during which the judge served in four different provinces of the T'ang Empire. From the suspected treason of a general in the Chinese army facing the Tartar hordes on the western frontier to the murder of a lonely poet in his garden pavilion in Han-yuan, the cases presented here are among the most memorable of Judge Dee's long and distinguished career.

BOOKS BY ROBERT VAN GULIK

The Emperor's Pearl
The Haunted Monastery
The Lacquer Screen
The Red Pavilion
The Willow Pattern
The Monkey and the Tiger
The Phantom of the Temple
Murder in Canton
Necklace and Calabash
Poets and Murder
Judge Dee at Work

JUDGE DEE AT WORK

Eight Chinese Detective Stories

by

ROBERT VAN GULIK

With illustrations
drawn by the author in Chinese style

Charles Scribner's Sons: New York

1 3 5 7 9 11 13 15 17 19 A/P 20 18 16 14 12 10 8 6 4 2

Printed in the United States of America
Library of Congress Catalog Card Number 72-1210
ISBN 684-16179-6

CONTENTS

ILLUSTRATIONS

FIVE AUSPICIOUS CLOUDS

This case occurred in A.D. 663 when Judge Dee had been serving only a week in his first independent official post— Magistrate of Peng-lai, a remote district on the north-east coast of the Chinese Empire. Directly upon his arrival there he had been confronted with three mysterious crimes, described in my novel The Chinese Gold Murders. *In that story mention was made of the flourishing shipbuilding industry of Peng-lai, and of Mr Yee Pen, the wealthy shipowner. The present story opens in Judge Dee's private office in the tribunal, where he is in conference with Yee Pen and two other gentlemen; they have just finished discussing at length Judge Dee's proposal for bringing the shipbuilding industry under government control.*

'Well, gentlemen,' Judge Dee said with a satisfied smile to his three guests, 'that settles it then, I think.'

The conference in his private office had begun at about two o'clock, and now it was already past five. But he thought that the time had been well spent.

'The rules we drafted seem to cover all possible contingencies,' Mr Ho remarked in his precise voice. He was a soberly dressed, middle-aged man, a retired secretary of the Minister of Justice. Looking at Hwa Min, the wealthy shipowner on his right, he added, 'You'll agree, Mr Hwa, that our draft provides for an equitable settlement of your differences with your colleague Mr Yee Pen here.'

Hwa Min made a face. ' "Equitable" is a nice word,' he said dryly, 'but as a merchant I like the word "profitable" even better ! If I had been given a free hand in competing with my friend Mr Yee, the result might not have been exactly equitable, no. . . . But it would have been eminently profitable—for me !'

'Shipbuilding affects our coastal defence,' Judge Dee observed stiffly. 'The Imperial Government does not allow a private monopoly. We have spent the entire afternoon on this matter and, thanks also to the excellent technical advice of Mr Ho, we have now drafted this document setting forth clearly the rules all ship-owners are to follow. I shall expect both of you to keep to those rules.'

Mr Yee Pen nodded ponderously. The judge liked this shrewd, but honest businessman. He thought less of Mr Hwa Min, who he knew was not averse to shady deals, and who often had woman-trouble. Judge Dee gave a sign to the clerk to refill the teacups, then he leaned back in his chair. It had been a hot day, but now a cool breeze had risen, wafting into the small office the scent of the magnolia tree outside the window.

Mr Yee set his cup down and gave Ho and Hwa Min a questioning look. It was time for them to take their leave.

Suddenly the door opened and Sergeant Hoong, Judge Dee's trusted old adviser, came in. He stepped up to the desk and said: 'There's someone outside with an urgent message, Your Honour.'

Judge Dee had caught his look. 'Excuse me for one moment,' he said to his three guests. He rose and followed the sergeant outside.

When they were standing in the corridor, the sergeant told him in a low voice, 'It's Mr Ho's house steward, sir. He came to report to his master that Mrs Ho has committed suicide.'

'Almighty heaven!' the judge exclaimed. 'Tell him to wait. I'd better break this bad news to Ho myself. How did she do it?'

'She hanged herself, Your Honour. In their garden pavilion, during the siesta. The steward came rushing out here at once.'

'Too bad for Mr Ho. I like the fellow. A bit on the dry side, but very conscientious. And a clever jurist.'

He sadly shook his head, then re-entered his office. After he had sat down again behind his desk, he addressed Ho gravely: 'It was your house steward, Mr Ho. He came with shocking news. About Mrs Ho.'

Ho grasped the armrests of his chair. 'About my wife?'

'It seems that she committed suicide, Mr Ho.'

Mr Ho half-rose, then let himself sink back again into his chair. He said in a toneless voice, 'So it happened, just as I feared. She . . . she was very depressed, these last weeks.' He passed his hand over his eyes, then asked: 'How . . . how did she do it, sir?'

'Your steward reported that she hanged herself. He is waiting now to take you home, Mr Ho. I'll send the coroner along at once, to draw up the death certificate. You will want to have the formalities over and done with as quickly as possible, of course.'

Mr Ho did not seem to have heard him. 'Dead!' he muttered. 'Only a few hours after I had left her! What shall I do?'

'We'll help you with everything of course, Mr Ho,' Hwa Min said consolingly. He added a few words of condolence, in which Yee Pen joined. But Ho did not seem to have heard them. He was staring into space, his face drawn. Suddenly he looked up at the judge and spoke after some hesitation:

'I need time, sir, a little time to . . . I don't like to presume upon your kindness, sir, but . . . would it perhaps be possible for Your Honour to get someone to attend to the formalities on my behalf? Then I can go home after . . . after the autopsy, and when the dead body has been . . .' He let his voice trail off, giving the judge a pleading look.

'Of course, Mr Ho!' Judge Dee replied briskly. 'You remain here and have another cup of tea. I'll go personally to your house with the coroner, and a temporary coffin will be prepared. It's the least I can do. You have never grudged me your valuable advice, and today again you have devoted your entire afternoon to the business of this tribunal. No, I insist, Mr Ho! You two look after our friend, gentlemen. I'll be back here in half an hour or so.'

Sergeant Hoong was waiting in the courtyard, together with a small rotund man with a black goatee. Hoong presented him as Ho's house steward. Judge Dee told him, 'I have informed Mr Ho already; you can return now, steward. I'll be along presently.' He added to Sergeant Hoong, 'You'd better go back to the chancery, Hoong, and sort out the official papers that have come in. We'll have a look at them together after I get back. Where are my two lieutenants?'

'Ma Joong and Chiao Tai are in the main courtyard, sir, putting the guards through their drill.'

'Good. I need only the headman and two of his men to go to

3

Mr Ho's house. They'll place the dead body in the coffin. When Ma Joong and Chiao Tai are through with the drill, they can retire. I shan't need them tonight. Get the coroner and have my official palankeen brought out!'

In the small front courtyard of Mr Ho's modest residence the small, obese steward stood waiting for the judge. Two red-eyed maids were hovering near the gatehouse. The headman helped Judge Dee to alight from his palankeen. The judge ordered him to wait with the two constables in the courtyard, then told the steward to conduct him and the coroner to the pavilion.

The small man led them along the open corridor that circled the house to an extensive garden, surrounded by a high wall. He took them down a well-kept path winding among the flowering shrubs to the farthest corner. There, in the shade of two tall oak trees, stood an octagonal pavilion, built on a round brick platform. The pointed, green-tiled roof was topped by a gilded globe, and the pillars and the intricate lattice-work of the windows were lacquered a bright red. The judge went up the four marble steps and pulled the door open.

It was hot in the small but high room, the pungent smell of some outlandish incense hung heavily in the close air. Judge Dee's eyes went at once to the bamboo couch against the wall on the right. The still figure of a woman was stretched out on it. The face was turned to the wall; he saw only the thick strands of glossy hair spilling out over her shoulders. She was clad in a summer robe of white silk, her small feet were shod in white satin shoes. Turning round to the coroner, Judge Dee said:

'You go ahead and examine her while I prepare the death certificate. Open the windows, steward, it is very stuffy in here.'

The judge took an official form from his sleeve and put it ready on the side table beside the door. Then he idly surveyed the room. On the centre table of carved rosewood stood a tea-tray with two cups. The square teapot had been knocked over; it was lying with its spout half across a flat brass box. A length of red silk cord was lying next to it. Two high-backed chairs stood by the table. Except for two racks of spotted bamboo between the windows, holding books and a few small antiques, there was no other furniture.

4

The upper half of the walls was covered with wooden tablets, inscribed with famous poems. There was an atmosphere of quiet, elegant taste.

The steward had pushed open the last window. Now he came up to the judge and pointed to the thick, red-lacquered beams running across the dome-shaped ceiling. From the central beam dangled a red cord, its end frayed.

'We found her hanging there, sir. The chambermaid and I.'

Judge Dee nodded. 'Was Mrs Ho depressed this morning?'

'Oh no, sir, she was in high spirits at the noon meal. But when Mr Hwa Min came to visit the master, she . . .'

'Hwa Min, you say? What did he come here for? He was going to meet Mr Ho in my office at two!'

The steward looked embarrassed. After some hesitation he replied, 'While I was serving tea to the two gentlemen in the reception room, sir, I couldn't help hearing what was being said. I understand that Mr Hwa wanted my master to give Your Honour advice during the conference that would be advantageous to him. He even offered my master a substantial ah . . . reward. My master refused indignantly, of course. . . .'

The coroner stepped up to the judge. 'I'd like to show Your Honour something rather odd!' he said.

Noticing the coroner's worried expression, Judge Dee ordered the steward curtly: 'Go and fetch Mrs Ho's chambermaid!' Then he went over to the couch. The coroner had turned the dead woman's head round. The face was badly distorted, but one could still see that she had been a handsome woman. The judge put her age at about thirty. The coroner pushed the hair aside and showed the judge a bad bruise above the left temple.

'This is one point that worries me, sir,' he said slowly. 'The second is that the death was caused by strangulation, but none of the vertebrae of the neck has been dislocated. Now I measured the length of the cord dangling from that beam up there, of the noose lying on the table and of the woman herself. It's easy to see how she could have done it. She stepped on that chair, then onto the table. She threw the cord over the beam, tied one end in a slip-knot and pulled it tight round the beam. Then she made the other end into a noose, put it round her neck and jumped

5

from the table, upsetting the teapot. While she was hanging there, her feet must have been only a few inches from the floor. The noose slowly strangled her, but her neck was not broken. I can't help wondering why she didn't put the other chair on the table, then jump down from it. A drop like that would have broken her neck, ensuring a quick death. If one combines this fact with the bruise on her temple. . .' He broke off and gave the judge a meaningful look.

'You are right,' Judge Dee said. He took the official form and put it back in his sleeve. Heaven only knew when he would be able to issue the death certificate! He sighed and asked: 'What about the time of death?'

'That's hard to say, Your Honour. The body is still warm, and the limbs haven't yet begun to stiffen. But in this hot weather, and in this closed room . . .'

The judge nodded absentmindedly. He was staring at the brass box. It had the shape of a pentagon with rounded corners, measuring about a foot in diameter, and about an inch high. The brass cover showed a cut-out design of five interconnected spirals. Through it one could see the brown powder that filled the box to the brim.

The coroner followed his glance. 'That's an incense-clock,' he remarked.

'It is indeed. The pattern excised in the cover is that of the Five Auspicious Clouds, each cloud being represented by one spiral. If one lights the incense at the beginning of the design, it'll slowly burn on along the spirals of the pattern, as if it were a fuse. Look, the tea spilling from the spout of the teapot moistened the centre of the third spiral, extinguishing the incense about halfway through that part of the design. If we could find out when exactly this incense-clock was lit, and how long it took the fire to reach the centre of the third spiral, we would be able to establish the approximate time of the suicide. Or rather of the . . .'

Judge Dee checked himself, for the steward had come in. He was accompanied by a portly woman of about fifty, in a neat brown dress. Her round face still showed traces of tears. As soon as she had seen the still figure on the couch, she burst out in sobs.

6

'How long has she been with Mrs Ho?' Judge Dee asked the steward.

'More than twenty years, Your Honour. She belonged to Mrs Ho's own family, and three years ago followed her here, after Mr Ho had married her. She is not too bright, but a good woman. The mistress was very fond of her.'

THE DESIGN OF THE INCENSE-CLOCK

'Calm yourself!' the judge addressed the maid. 'This must be a terrible shock for you, but if you answer my questions promptly, we'll be able to have the body properly placed in a coffin very soon. Tell me, are you familiar with this incense-clock?'

She wiped her face with her sleeve and replied listlessly, 'Of course I am, sir. It burns exactly five hours, each spiral taking one hour. Just before I left, the mistress complained of the musty air here, and I lit the incense.'

7

'What time was that?'

'It was getting on for two, sir.'

'That was the last time you saw your mistress alive, wasn't it?'

'Yes, sir. When Mr Hwa was talking with the master in the reception room, over in the house, I took my mistress here. Soon after the master came in, to see that she was comfortably established for her siesta. She told me to pour two cups of tea, adding that she wouldn't need me again until five o'clock, and that I'd better take a nap also. She was always so considerate! I went back to the house and told the steward to lay out in the main bedroom the master's new grey dress, for the conference in the tribunal. Then the master came too. After the steward had helped him to change, the master told me to fetch Mr Hwa. They left the house together.'

'Where was Mr Hwa?'

'I found him in the garden, sir, admiring the flowers.'

'That's right,' the steward remarked. 'After the conversation in the reception room I just told Your Honour about, the master asked Mr Hwa to excuse him while he said good-bye to Mrs Ho in the pavilion and changed. It seems that Mr Hwa, left alone in the reception room, got bored and went outside to have a look at the garden.'

'I see. Now who discovered the body first, you or this maid?'

'I did, sir,' the maid replied. 'I came here a little before five o'clock, and I . . . I saw her hanging there, from that beam. I rushed out and called the steward.'

'I stood on the chair at once,' the steward said, 'and cut the cord while the maid put her arms round her. I prised the cord loose, and then we carried her to the couch. Breathing and heartbeat had stopped. We tried to revive her with vigorous massage, but it was too late. I hurried to the tribunal to report to the master. If I had discovered her earlier . . .'

'You did what you could, steward. Let me see now. You told me that during the noon meal Mrs Ho was in high spirits, until the arrival of Mr Hwa, right?'

'Yes, sir. When Mrs Ho heard me announce Mr Hwa's arrival to the master, she turned pale and quickly withdrew to the side room. I saw that she . . .'

'You must be mistaken!' the maid interrupted crossly. 'I accompanied her when she went from the side room to the pavilion, and I didn't notice that she was upset!'

The steward was about to make an angry retort, but Judge Dee held up his hand and said curtly to him: 'Go to the gatehouse, and ask the gatekeeper what persons he admitted to the house after your master and Mr Hwa had left—why they came and how long they stayed. Hurry up!'

When the steward had scurried away, Judge Dee sat down at the table. Slowly caressing his sidewhiskers, he silently studied the woman who was standing in front of him with downcast eyes. Then he spoke: 'Your mistress is dead. It is your duty to tell us everything that might help to find the person who either directly or indirectly caused her death. Speak up, why did the arrival of Mr Hwa distress her?'

The maid darted a frightened look at him. She replied diffidently: 'I really don't know, sir! I only know that in the past two weeks she went twice to visit Mr Hwa, without Mr Ho knowing it. I wanted to go with her, but Mr Fung said . . .' She suddenly broke off. Growing red in the face, she angrily bit her lip.

'Who is Mr Fung?' Judge Dee asked sharply.

She deliberated for a while, her forehead creased in a deep frown. Then she shrugged her shoulders and answered, 'Well, it's bound to come out, and they didn't do anything wrong anyway! Mr Fung is a painter, sir, very poor and in bad health. He used to live in a small hovel near our house. Six years ago the father of my mistress, the retired prefect, engaged Mr Fung to teach my mistress to paint flowers. She was only twenty-two then, and he was such a handsome young man. . . . No wonder they fell in love with each other. Mr Fung is such a nice man, Your Honour, and his father was a famous scholar. But he lost all his money, and . . .'

'Never mind that! Were they lovers?'

The maid shook her head emphatically and replied quickly, 'Never, sir! Mr Fung had planned to ask somebody to approach the old prefect regarding a marriage. It's true that he was desperately poor, but since he belonged to such an illustrious family

9

here was hope that the prefect would consent. Just at that time, however, Mr Fung's cough grew worse. He consulted a physician and was told that he was suffering from an incurable lung disease, and would die young. . . . Mr Fung told her that they could never marry, it had all been but a brief dream of spring. He would go away to a distant place. But she implored him to stay; she said they could still remain friends, and that she wanted to be near him should the disease grow worse. . . .'

'Did they continue to meet after Mr Ho had married your mistress?'

'Yes, sir. Here in the pavilion. But only during the daytime, and I was always there. I swear that he never even touched her hand, sir!'

'Did Mr Ho know about those visits?'

'No, of course not! We would wait till the master was away for the day, then I would take a note from my mistress to Mr Fung, and he would slip inside by the garden door and have a cup of tea with her here in the pavilion. I know these occasional visits were the only thing that kept Mr Fung going, all through the last three years, after my mistress married. And she enjoyed their talks so much! And I was there, always. . . .'

'You connived at clandestine meetings,' the judge said harshly. 'And probably at murder. For your mistress did not commit suicide, she was killed. At half past four, to be precise.'

'But how could Mr Fung have anything to do with that, Your Honour?' the maid wailed.

'That's what I am going to find out,' the judge said grimly. He turned to the coroner. 'Let's go to the gatehouse!'

The headman and his two constables were sitting on the stone bench in the front courtyard. Springing to attention, the headman saluted and asked, 'Shall I tell my men to fetch a temporary coffin, sir?'

'No, not yet,' the judge said gruffly, and walked on.

In the doorkeeper's lodge the small steward was cursing a wizened old man in a long blue gown. Two grinning palankeen-bearers were looking inside through the window, and listening with relish.

'This man maintains that nobody came to the house, Your Honour,' the steward said angrily. 'But the old fool confessed that he took a nap between three and four. Disgraceful!'

Disregarding this remark, the judge asked abruptly: 'Do you know a painter called Fung?'

The astonished steward shook his head, but the elder coolie called out, 'I know Mr Fung, Excellency! He often buys a bowl of noodles at my father's stall round the corner. He rents an attic over the grocery, behind this house. I saw him standing about near our garden gate an hour or so ago.'

Judge Dee turned to the coroner and said: 'Let this coolie take you to Mr Fung's place, and bring him here. On no account let Mr Fung know about Mrs Ho's demise!' Then he ordered the steward: 'Lead me to the reception room. I shall see Mr Fung there.'

The reception room proved to be rather small, but the simple furniture was of good quality. The steward offered the judge a comfortable armchair at the centre table, and poured him a cup of tea. Then he discreetly withdrew.

Slowly sipping the tea, Judge Dee reflected with satisfaction that the murderer had now been traced. He hoped the coroner would find the painter in, so that he could interrogate him at once.

Sooner than he had expected the coroner entered with a tall, thin man of about thirty, clad in a threadbare but clean blue robe, fastened with a black cotton sash. He had a rather distinguished face, with a short black moustache. A few locks of hair came out from under the faded black cap he was wearing. The judge took in his large, rather too brilliant eyes, and the red spots on the hollow cheeks. He motioned him to take the chair on the other side of the table. The coroner poured a cup of tea for the guest, then remained standing behind his chair.

'I have heard about your work, Mr Fung,' the judge began affably. 'I have been looking forward to making your acquaintance.'

The painter straightened his robe with a long, sensitive hand. Then he spoke in a cultured voice: 'I feel most flattered by your interest, sir. Yet I find it hard to believe that Your Honour ur-

11

gently summoned me here to Mr Ho's house just to engage in a leisurely talk about artistic matters.'

'Not in the first place, no. An accident has occurred in the garden here, Mr Fung, and I am looking for witnesses.'

Fung sat up in his chair. He asked worriedly: 'An accident? Not involving Mrs Ho, I trust?'

'It did indeed involve her, Mr Fung. It occurred between four and five, in the pavilion. And you came to see her at that time.'

'What has happened to her?' the painter burst out.

'You ought to know the answer to that yourself!' Judge Dee said coldly. 'For it was you who murdered her!'

'She is dead!' Fung exclaimed. He buried his face in his hands. His narrow shoulders were shaking. When after a long time he looked up, he had himself under control again. He asked in a measured voice: 'Would you kindly inform me, sir, why I should have murdered the woman I loved more than anything else in the world?'

'Your motive was fear of exposure. After her marriage you continued to force your attentions on her. She grew tired of it and told you that if you didn't stop seeing her she would inform her husband. Today you two had a violent quarrel, and you killed her.'

The painter nodded slowly. 'Yes,' he said resignedly, 'that would be a plausible explanation, I suppose. And I was indeed at the garden gate at the time you mentioned.'

'Did she know you were coming?'

'Yes. This morning a street urchin brought me a note from her. It said that she had to see me, on an urgent matter. If I would come at about half past four to the garden gate, and knock four times as usual, the maid would let me in.'

'What happened after you had gone inside?'

'I didn't go inside. I knocked several times, but the gate remained closed. I walked up and down there for a while, and having made one more fruitless attempt, I went back home.'

'Show me her note!'

'I can't, for I destroyed it. As she told me to.'

'So you deny having killed her?'

Fung shrugged his shoulders. 'If you are certain that you won't be able to discover the real criminal, sir, I am perfectly willing to say I killed her, just to help you dispose of the case. I'll be dead before long anyway, and whether I die in bed or on the scaffold is all the same to me. Her death has robbed me of my last reason for prolonging this miserable life. For my other love, my art, has already left me long ago—this lingering illness seems to destroy the creative impulse. If, on the other hand, you think it possible to trace the cruel fiend who murdered this innocent woman, then there's no earthly reason why I should confuse the issue by confessing to a crime I did not commit.'

Judge Dee gave him a long look, pensively tugging at his moustache. 'Was Mrs Ho in the habit of sending you her messages through a street urchin?'

'No, sir. Her maid always brought the notes, and this was the first time it contained the request to burn it. But it was hers all right, I am familiar with her style and her handwriting.' A violent attack of coughing interrupted him. He wiped his mouth with a paper handkerchief, looked for a moment indifferently at the flecks of blood, then resumed, 'I can't imagine what urgent matter she wanted to discuss. And who would have wanted her dead? I have known her and her family for more than ten years, and I can assure you that they didn't have an enemy in the world!' Fingering his moustache, he added, 'Her marriage was a reasonably happy one. Ho is a bit dull, but he is genuinely fond of her, always kind and considerate. Never spoke of taking a concubine, although she hadn't born him a child. And she liked and respected him.'

'Which did not prevent her from continuing to meet you behind his back!' the judge remarked dryly. 'Most reprehensible behaviour for a married woman. Not to mention you!'

The painter gave him a haughty look.

'You wouldn't understand,' he said coldly. 'You are caught in a net of empty rules and meaningless conventions. There was nothing reprehensible about our friendship, I tell you. The only reason we kept our meetings secret was because Ho is a rather old-fashioned man who would interpret our relations as wrongly as you seem to do. We didn't want to hurt him.'

'Most considerate of you! Since you knew Mrs Ho so

well, you can doubtless tell me why she was often depressed of late?'

'Oh yes. The fact is that her father, the old prefect, didn't manage his finances too well, and got deeply in debt with that wealthy shipowner Hwa Min. Since a month or so that heartless usurer has been pressing the old man to transfer his land to him, in lieu of payment, but the prefect wants to keep it. It has belonged to his family for heaven knows how many generations, and moreover he feels responsible for the welfare of the tenant farmers. Hwa would squeeze the last copper out of those poor devils! The old man begged Hwa to wait till after the harvest, then he'd be able to pay Hwa at least the atrocious interest due. But Hwa insists on foreclosing, so as to get that land into his hands cheaply. Mrs Ho kept worrying about this affair, she made me take her to see Hwa twice. She did her best to persuade him to drop his demand for immediate payment, but the dirty rat said he would consider that only if she let him sleep with her!'

'Did Mr Ho know about those visits?'

'He didn't. We knew how much it would distress him to hear that his father-in-law was in financial trouble while he could do nothing to help him. Mr Ho has no private means, you know. He has to depend on his modest pension for his living.'

'You two were indeed very kind towards Mr Ho!'

'He deserved it; he is a decent fellow. The only thing he couldn't give his wife was intellectual companionship, and that she found in me.'

'I never saw such a complete lack of the most elementary morality!' the judge exclaimed disgustedly. He got up and ordered the coroner: 'Hand this man over to the headman, to be locked up in jail as a murder suspect. Thereafter you and the two constables convey Mrs Ho's dead body to the tribunal, and conduct a thorough autopsy. Report to me as soon as you are through. You'll find me in my private office.'

He left, angrily shaking his long sleeves.

Mr Ho and the two shipowners were waiting in Judge Dee's private office, attended upon by a clerk. They wanted to rise when the judge came in, but he motioned them to remain seated. He took the armchair behind his desk, and told the clerk to refill the teacups.

'Has everything been settled, Your Honour?' Mr Ho asked in a dull voice.

Judge Dee emptied his cup, then rested his forearms on the desk and replied slowly, 'Not quite, Mr Ho. I have bad news for you. I found that your wife did not commit suicide. She was murdered.'

Mr Ho uttered a suppressed cry. Mr Hwa and Mr Yee exchanged an astonished look. Then Ho blurted out, 'Murdered? Who did it? And why, in the name of heaven?'

'The evidence points to a painter, by the name of Fung.'

'Fung? A painter? Never heard of him!'

'I warned you the news was bad, Mr Ho. Very bad. Before you married your wife, she had friendly relations with this painter. After the marriage the two kept on seeing each other secretly, in the garden pavilion. It is possible that she grew tired of him and wanted to end the liaison. Knowing that you would be here all afternoon, she may have sent Fung a note asking him to come and see her. And if she then told him that they were through, he may well have killed her.'

Ho sat there staring straight ahead, his thin lips compressed. Yee and Hwa looked embarrassed; they made to get up and leave the judge and Ho alone. But Judge Dee gave them a peremptory sign to stay where they were. At last Mr Ho looked up and asked: 'How did the villain kill her?'

'She was knocked unconscious by a blow on her temple, then strung up by the neck to a beam and strangled. The murderer upset a teapot, and the tea from it extinguished the fire of the incense-clock, establishing half past four or thereabouts as the time he committed his evil deed. I may add that a witness saw the painter Fung loitering about at that time near your garden gate.'

There was a knock on the door. The coroner came in and handed a document to the judge. Quickly glancing through the autopsy report, he saw that the cause of death had indeed been slow strangulation. Beyond the bruise on the temple the body bore no other marks of violence. She had been in the third month of pregnancy.

Judge Dee folded the paper up slowly and put it into his sleeve. Then he said to the coroner, 'Tell the headman to set free the man he put in jail. That person will have to wait a while in the guard-room, though. I may want to question him again later.'

When the coroner had left, Mr Ho got up. He said in a hoarse voice, 'If Your Honour will allow me, I'll now take my leave. I must . . .'

'Not yet, Mr Ho,' the judge interrupted. 'I want to ask you a question first. Here in front of Mr Hwa and Mr Yee.'

Ho sat down again with a perplexed look.

'You left your wife in the pavilion at about two o'clock, Mr Ho,' Judge Dee resumed. 'And you were here in this office till five, when your steward came to report your wife's demise. For all we know she could have died any time between two and five. Yet when I told you about her suicide you said: "Only a few hours after I had left her . . ." as Mr Hwa and Mr Yee here will attest. How did you know that she died at about half past four?'

Ho made no answer. He stared at the judge with wide, un-believing eyes. Judge Dee went on, his voice suddenly harsh:

'I'll tell you! Because when you had killed your wife at two o'clock, directly after the maid had left the pavilion, you inten-tionally spilled the tea over the incense-clock. You apparently consider me a fairly competent investigator—thank you. You knew that if I visited the scene I would discover that your wife had been murdered, and deduct from the incense-clock that the deed had been done at about half past four. You also assumed that I would find out sooner or later that Fung had been at the garden gate at about that time—lured there by the faked note you had sent him. It was a clever scheme, Ho, worthy of an expert in juridical affairs. But the carefully faked time element proved to be your undoing. You kept telling yourself: I can never be suspected, because the time of the murder is clearly established at half past four. And so you inadvertently made that slip about "a few hours after I had left her". At that time the remark didn't strike me as odd. But as soon as I realized that if Fung was not the murderer it had to be you, I remembered those

16

words, and that provided the final proof of your guilt. The Five Auspicious Clouds didn't prove very auspicious for you, Mr Ho!'

Ho righted himself. He asked coldly: 'Why should I want to murder my wife?'

'I'll tell you. You had found out about her secret meetings with Fung, and when she told you she was pregnant you decided to destroy them both, with one and the same blow. You assumed that Fung was the father of the unborn child and . . .'

'He was not!' Ho suddenly shrieked. 'Do you think that miserable wretch could ever have . . . No, it was *my* child, do you hear? The only thing those two were capable of was sickening, sentimental drivel! And all the kind words I overheard them saying about me! . . . the decent but rather dull husband, who was entitled to her body, mind you, but who could of course never understand her sublime mind. I could, I could have . . .' He began to stutter in impotent rage. Then he took hold of himself and went on in a calmer voice, 'I didn't want the child of a woman with the mind of a streetwalker, a woman who . . .'

'That'll do!' Judge Dee said curtly. He clapped his hands. When the headman came in he said, 'Put this murderer into chains and lock him up. I shall hear his full confession tomorrow, in the tribunal.'

After the headman had led Ho away, the judge continued to Yee Pen, 'The clerk shall see you out, Mr Yee.' Turning to the other shipowner, he added, 'As for you, Mr Hwa, you'll stay a few moments: I want a word with you in private.'

When the two men were alone, Hwa said unctuously, 'Your Honour solved this crime in a remarkably short time! To think that Ho . . .' He sadly shook his head.

Judge Dee gave him a sour look. 'I was not too happy with Fung as a suspect,' he remarked dryly. 'The evidence against him fitted too neatly together, while the manner of the murder was totally inconsistent with his personality. I made my palankeen bearers bring me back here by a roundabout way, so as to have a little time to think. I reasoned that since the evidence could only have been rigged by an insider, it had to be Ho—the well-known motive of the deceived husband who wants to take vengeance on his adulterous wife and her lover, both at the same

17

time. But why did Ho wait so long? He knew everything about Mrs Ho sending messages to Fung; he must have discovered all about their secret meetings long ago. When I saw from the autopsy report that Mrs Ho had been pregnant, I took it that it was this news that had made her husband resolve to act. And I was right, though we now know that his emotional reaction was different from what I had assumed.' Fixing the shipowner with his sombre eyes, he continued, 'The false evidence could have been fabricated only by an insider, familiar with the incense-clock and with Mrs Ho's handwriting. That saved you from being accused of this murder, Mr Hwa!'

'Me, sir?' Hwa exclaimed aghast.

'Of course. I knew about Mrs Ho's visits to you, and about her refusing your disgusting proposal. Her husband was ignorant of this, but Fung knew. That gave you a motive for wanting both her and Fung out of the way. And you also had the opportunity, for you were in the garden towards two o'clock, while Mrs Ho was alone in the pavilion. You are innocent of murder, Mr Hwa, but guilty of attempted seduction of a married woman, as will be attested by Mr Fung, and of attempted bribery, as will be attested by Ho's steward, who overheard your conversation while you were visiting Ho at noon. Tomorrow I shall charge you with these two offences in the tribunal, and sentence you to a term in prison. That will be the end of your career here in Peng-lai, Mr Hwa.'

Hwa jumped up and was about to kneel down and beg for mercy, but Judge Dee went on quickly:

'I shan't have you up on those two charges, provided you agree to pay two fines. First, you shall this very night write a formal letter to Mrs Ho's father, duly signed and sealed, informing him that he can pay back the money you lent him any time that suits him, and that you renounce all interest on that loan. Second, you shall commission Mr Fung to paint a picture of every single boat in your shipyard, paying him one silver piece for each drawing.' He cut short Hwa's protestations of gratitude by raising his hand. 'This fine gets you only a reprieve, of course. As soon as I hear that you are again importuning decent women, you shall be indicted on the charges mentioned. Go now to the guardroom. You'll find Mr Fung there, and you'll place your order with him.

Pay him then and there five silver pieces as an advance. Good-bye!'

When the frightened shipowner had hurriedly taken his leave, the judge got up from his chair and went to stand in front of the open window. He enjoyed the subtle fragrance of the magnolia blossoms for a while, then he muttered to himself: 'Disapproval of a man's moral standards is no reason for one to allow him to die in misery!'

He turned round abruptly and left for the chancery.

THE RED TAPE MURDER

*The coastal district of Peng-lai, where Judge Dee began his
career as a magistrate, was jointly administered by the judge,
in his capacity as the highest local civil servant, and by the
commander of the Imperial Army unit stationed there. The
extent of their respective jurisdiction was fairly clearly laid
down; civilian and military affairs seldom overlapped. When
Judge Dee had been serving in Peng-lai for just over a month,
however, he was drawn unexpectedly into a purely military
affair. My novel* The Chinese Gold Murders *mentions the
large fort, three miles downstream from the city of Peng-lai,
which was built at the mouth of the river to prevent the land-
ings of the Korean navy. It was within the walls of this
formidable stronghold that the military murder described in
this story took place: a proper men's affair, with no ladies
present—but featuring yards and yards of red tape!*

Judge Dee looked up from the file he was leafing through and
peevishly addressed the two men on the other side of his desk:
'Can't you two sit still? Stop fidgeting, will you?'

As the judge turned to his file again his two hefty lieutenants,
Ma Joong and Chiao Tai, made a determined effort to keep still
on their stools. Soon, however, Ma Joong stealthily gave Chiao
Tai an encouraging nod. The latter placed his large hands on his
knees and opened his mouth to speak. But just then the judge
pushed the file away and exclaimed disgustedly:

'This is most annoying; document P-404 is indeed missing! For
a moment I thought that Sergeant Hoong must have inserted it
in the wrong folder, since he was in rather a hurry yesterday
before he left for the prefecture. But P-404 simply isn't there!'

'Couldn't it be in the second file, Magistrate?' Ma Joong asked.
'That folder is also marked with the letter P.'

'Nonsense!' Judge Dee snapped. 'Haven't I explained to you
that in the archives of the fort they have two files marked P, P
for Personnel and P for Purchases? In the latter file, paper P-405

20

concerning a purchase of leather belts is clearly marked: "Refer back to P-404". That proves beyond doubt that P-404 belongs to Purchases, and not to Personnel.'

'This red tape business is a bit beyond me, sir! Besides, those two P files contain only information-copies sent on to us by the fort. Now as regards the fort, sir, we . . .'

'This is *not* mere red tape,' Judge Dee interrupted him sourly. 'It concerns the close observation of an established office routine, without which the entire administrative machinery of our Empire would get clogged.' Noticing the unhappy look on the deeply-tanned faces of his two lieutenants, the judge smiled despite himself and went on in a more friendly tone, 'In the four weeks that you two have been working for me here in Peng-lai, you have proved yourselves able to deal efficiently with the rough work. But the task of an officer of the tribunal comprises more than the arrest of dangerous criminals. He must keep abreast of the office routine, harbour a feeling for its finer points, and realize the importance of adhering to those finer points—a practice sometimes referred to by ignorant outsiders as red-tapery. Now this missing paper P-404 may well be quite unimportant in itself. But the fact that it is missing makes it of supreme importance.'

Folding his arms in his wide sleeves, he continued, 'Ma Joong correctly observed that these two files marked P contain nothing but copies, namely of the correspondence of the fort with the Board of Military Affairs in the capital. Those papers deal with purely military matters that don't concern us directly. What does concern us, however, is that every single file in this tribunal, whether important or unimportant, must be kept in good order, and must above all be complete!' Raising his forefinger for emphasis, the judge went on, 'Remember now, once and for all: you must be able to rely unreservedly on your files, and you can do so only when you are absolutely sure they are complete. An incomplete file has no place in a well-run office. An incomplete file is worthless!'

'Let's heave that P-file out of the window, then!' Ma Joong exclaimed. Then he added quickly: 'Beg your pardon, sir, but the fact is that Brother Chiao and I are rather upset. This morning we heard that our best friend here, Colonel Meng Kwo-tai, was found guilty last night of having murdered Colonel Soo, the Vice-Commander of the fort.'

Judge Dee straightened himself. 'So you two know Meng, eh? I heard about that murder the day before yesterday. Since I was very busy writing the report Hoong took to the capital, I didn't make inquiries. Anyway it's a military case that exclusively concerns the commander of the fort. How did you two come to know Colonel Meng?'

'Well,' Ma Joong replied, 'a couple of weeks ago we ran into him in a wine-house when he was spending his evening off here in town. The fellow is a fine athlete, excellent boxer, and the fort's champion archer. We became fast friends, and he made it a practice to spend all his free evenings with us. And now they say he shot the Vice-Commander! Of all the silly nonsense . . .'

'Don't worry,' Chiao Tai comforted his friend. 'Our magistrate'll straighten it all out!'

'It was like this, sir,' Ma Joong began eagerly. 'Day before yesterday the Vice-Commander . . .'

Judge Dee stopped him by raising his hand.

'In the first place,' he said dryly, 'I can't meddle with the affairs of the fort. Second, even if I could, I wouldn't be interested in hearsay of the murder. However, since you know the accused, you may as well tell me something more about him, for my orientation.'

'Colonel Meng is an upright, straightforward fellow!' Ma Joong burst out. 'We have boxed with him, got drunk with him and gone wenching with him. Let me tell you, Magistrate, that that's the way to get to know a man inside out! Now Vice-Commander Soo was a martinet and a bully, and Meng got his share of his foul mouth. I can imagine that some day Meng might fly into a rage and strike Soo down. But Meng would give himself up at once, and face the consequences. To shoot a man in his sleep, then deny he did it . . . No, sir, Meng wouldn't do that. Never!'

'Do you happen to know how Commander Fang feels about it?' the judge asked. 'He presided at the court martial, I presume.'

'He did,' Chiao Tai replied. 'And he confirmed the verdict of premeditated murder. Fang is a haughty, taciturn fellow. But rumour has it that he isn't too happy about the verdict—despite the fact that all the evidence points straight to Meng. Goes to show how popular the man is, even with his commanding officer!'

'When did you two last see Meng?' Judge Dee asked.

'The very night before Soo was murdered,' Ma Joong said. 'We had our supper together in the crab restaurant on the quay. Later that night two Korean merchants joined us, and the five of us had a real good drinking bout. It was long past midnight when Brother Chiao dropped Meng at the military barge that was to take him back to the fort.'

Judge Dee sat back in his chair and slowly tugged at his long sidewhiskers. Ma Joong quickly rose and poured him a cup of tea. The judge took a few sips, then he set his cup down and said briskly:

'I haven't yet returned Commander Fang's courtesy call. It's still early in the morning; if we leave now we'll be at the fort well before the noon rice. Tell the headman to have my official palankeen ready in the courtyard to carry us to the quay. In the meantime I'll change into ceremonial dress.' He got up from his chair. Seeing the satisfied looks of his two lieutenants, he added, 'I must warn you that I can't force my assistance on the Commander. If he doesn't ask for my advice, then that's the end of it. In any case I'll take the opportunity to ask him for an extra copy of that missing document.'

The sturdy rowers drove the heavy military barge to the north of the river in less than an hour. On the low bank to the left rose the forbidding walls of the fortress; ahead was the muddy water of the estuary, broadening out into the wide expanse of sunlit sea beyond.

Ma Joong and Chiao Tai jumped onto the quay under the towering front gate. When the captain of the guard discovered Judge Dee's identity, he at once took him across the paved courtyard to the main building. Ma Joong and Chiao Tai stayed behind in the gatehouse, for the judge had instructed them to pick up any gossip about the sensational murder.

Before stepping inside, Judge Dee cast an admiring glance at the thick, solid walls. The fort had been built only a few years before, when Korea had revolted against the T'ang Empire, and her fleet was preparing to invade China's north-east coast. The revolt had been crushed in two difficult campaigns by a Chinese expeditionary force, but the Koreans were still smarting from their defeat, and the possibility of a surprise attack had to be reckoned with. The river-mouth, and the fort guarding it, had been declared an emergency zone, and although it was located inside Peng-lai, Judge Dee had no authority in this particular area.

Commander Fang came to meet him at the bottom of the stairs, and took him up to his private office. He made the judge sit down by his side on the large couch against the back wall.

Fang was just as formal and sparing of words as when he had come to call on Judge Dee in the tribunal of Peng-lai. He sat stiffly erect, encased in his heavy coat of mail with the iron breast- and shoulder-pieces. Looking morosely at the judge from under his grey, tufted eyebrows, he brought out haltingly a few words of thanks for the visit.

Judge Dee made the usual polite inquiries. The Commander replied gruffly that he still thought his present post unsuitable for an old combat soldier. He didn't think the Koreans would start making trouble again; it would take them years to recoup their losses. And in the meantime he, Fang, had to keep order among more than a thousand officers and men cooped up idle in the fort.

The judge expressed his sympathy, then added, 'I hear that a murder occurred here recently. The criminal has been found and convicted, but I am eager to hear more about the case. As you know, Peng-lai is my first post, and I would welcome an opportunity to enlarge my experience.'

The Commander gave him a sharp look. He fingered his short grey moustache for a moment, then he got up abruptly and said curtly:

'Come along, I'll show you where and how it happened.'

While passing the two orderlies who stood stiffly at attention by the door, he barked at them:

'Get me Mao and Shih Lang!'

The Commander led the way across the inner courtyard to a large, two-storeyed building. As they ascended the broad staircase, he muttered, 'Case worries me, to tell you the truth!' At the head of the stairs four soldiers were sitting on a bench. They sprang to attention. The Commander guided Judge Dee down the long, empty corridor to the left. It ended at a heavy door; over its lock was pasted a strip of paper bearing the Commander's seal. Fang tore it off, kicked the door open and said:

'This was Vice-Commander Soo's room. He was murdered on the couch over there.'

Before crossing the threshold, the judge quickly surveyed the spacious, bare room. On his right was an open window arch, about five foot high and seven foot broad. In the recess below it lay a quiver of lacquered leather, containing a dozen or so iron-tipped arrows with red shafts. Four more had spilled out of the quiver. The room had no other window or door. On the left stood a simple desk of scarred, unpainted wood, on which lay an iron helmet and another arrow. Against the back wall stood a large bamboo couch. The reed mat covering it was stained with ominous, brownish spots. The floor consisted of roughly hewn boards; there was no rug or floor mat.

After they had gone inside, the Commander said:

'Soo used to come up here every afternoon about one o'clock, after drill, to take a brief nap till two, when he would go down to the officers' mess for the noon rice. Day before yesterday Colonel Shih Lang, who assists Soo with the administrative paperwork, comes up here a little before two. Planned to go down to the mess together with Soo, and have a few words with him in private about a breach of discipline concerning a Lieutenant Kao. Shih Lang knocks. No answer, so he thinks maybe Soo has gone down already. He steps inside to make sure, and sees Soo lying on that couch over there. He has his mail jacket on, but an arrow is sticking out of his unprotected stomach, and his leather trousers are covered with blood. Soo's hands are round the arrow's shaft —apparently he made a vain attempt to pull it out. But the tip is barbed, you see. Soo's as dead as a doornail.'

The Commander cleared his throat, then went on, 'You see what happened, don't you? Soo comes in here, throws his quiver in that recess, his helmet on that desk, then lies down on the couch, doesn't bother to take off his mail jacket or his boots. When he has dozed off . . .'

Two men entered and saluted smartly. The Commander motioned the tall man in the brown-leather uniform to step forward and grunted:

'This is Colonel Shih Lang, who discovered the body.'

Judge Dee took in Shih Lang's heavy, deeply lined face, his broad shoulders and long ape-like arms. He wore a short moustache and ring-beard. His lacklustre eyes stared sullenly at the judge.

Indicating the squat man who wore the short mail jacket, pointed helmet and baggy trousers of the mounted military police, the Commander added: 'And this is Colonel Mao, who was in charge of the investigation. Used to be my chief of military intelligence during the Korea campaign. Able fellow.'

The judge made a perfunctory bow. He thought Mao's thin, cynical face had a rather foxy expression.

'I was just explaining the facts to the magistrate here,' Commander Fang told the two men. 'Thought we might as well have his opinion.'

The two newcomers remained silent. Then Colonel Shih Lang broke the awkward pause. He said in a deep, rather hoarse voice, 'I hope the magistrate'll find another solution. In my opinion Meng is not a murderer. Let alone one who foully shoots a man in his sleep.'

'Opinions don't matter,' the military police chief remarked dryly. 'We only deal with facts. And on that basis we reached a unanimous verdict of guilty.'

The Commander hitched up his sword belt. He took Judge Dee to the large window arch and pointed at the three-storeyed building opposite. 'The ground floor and the second floor across the yard there have no windows—our storerooms are located there. But do you see that big window up on the top floor? That's the armoury.'

Judge Dee saw that the window indicated was of the same type and size as the one he was standing at. The Commander turned round and resumed, 'Now then, Soo was lying with his feet pointing towards this window. Experiments with a straw dummy proved that the arrow must have been shot from the window up in the armoury there. And at that time there was no one there but Colonel Meng.'

'Quite a distance,' Judge Dee remarked. 'About sixty feet, I'd say.'

'Colonel Meng is our champion archer,' Mao observed.

'Not a job for a beginner,' Commander Fang admitted, 'but quite feasible for an expert with the crossbow.'

The judge nodded. After a few moments' thought he asked, 'The arrow couldn't have been shot from within this room, I suppose?'

'No,' the Commander replied curtly. 'Four soldiers stand guard day and night at the head of the stairs, at the other end of the corridor. They testified that after Soo had come up here and before Shih Lang's arrival, no one passed them.'

'Couldn't the murderer have scaled the wall, entered through the window and stabbed Soo with the arrow?' Judge Dee asked. 'I am just trying to cover all possibilities,' he added quickly as he saw the pitying looks of the others.

'The wall is perfectly smooth, no human could ever scale it,' Fang said. 'Not even Shih Lang here, and he is our expert in that art. Besides, there are always soldiers about in the yard below, so nobody could perform antics on the wall unnoticed.'

'I see,' Judge Dee said. He stroked his long black beard, then asked: 'Why should Colonel Meng want to kill the Vice-Commander?'

'Soo was an able officer, but short-tempered and a bit rough in the mouth. Four days ago he cursed Meng in front of the troops, because Meng had taken sides with Lieutenant Kao.'

'I was present,' Mao said. 'Meng kept himself under control, but his face was livid. He brooded over this insult, and . . .' He paused significantly.

'Meng had been bawled out by Soo before,' Shih Lang remarked. 'He was accustomed to it, didn't take it seriously.'

Judge Dee said to the Commander: 'You mentioned this breach of discipline by Lieutenant Kao before. What did he do?'

'Soo cursed Kao because his leather belt was cracked. Kao

27

answered back and Soo was going to have him severely punished. Colonel Meng spoke up for Kao, and then Soo went for Meng.'

'I was going to put in a word for Kao too,' Shih Lang said. 'That's why I came up here, directly after the morning drill. I thought that if I talked to Soo privately, I could make him drop the case. And to think that fate ordained Kao as the main witness against Colonel Meng, his protector!'

'How was that?' the judge asked.

Commander Fang sighed. 'Everybody knew that Soo always used to come up here for a nap after the morning drill. And Colonel Meng was in the habit of going up to the armoury to exercise with the heavy spear before going down to the mess hall. Fellow is as strong as an ox, doesn't know the word fatigue. But day before yesterday Meng tells his colleagues that he has a hangover, he's not going up to the armoury after drill. Yet Meng did go! Look, do you see that smaller window up there, about twenty feet to the left of the armoury window? Well, that belongs to a room where leather goods are stored. Only the quartermaster goes up there, and only once in a fortnight or so. But Kao gets it into his head to look for a new leather belt there, because Soo had reprimanded him so severely about his old one. The fastidious beggar takes quite a time selecting a belt he likes. When he turns to the door connecting the room with the armoury, he happens to look out of the window. He sees Shih Lang enter Soo's room here. Shih Lang suddenly halts in his tracks right in front of the window arch, stoops, then starts waving his hands and rushes out of the room, shouting. Kao opens the door of the armoury to run down and find out what's wrong in the building opposite, and nearly collides with Colonel Meng, who is standing there fiddling with a crossbow. Both men rush down together and come up here directly behind the soldiers of the guard, who have been alarmed by Shih Lang. Then Shih Lang fetches me and Colonel Mao. When we arrive here, we know at once where that arrow came from, and I place Meng under arrest as the most likely suspect.'

'What about Lieutenant Kao?' Judge Dee asked.

Mao silently took him to the window and pointed outside.

Judge Dee looked up and realized that though from the window of the storeroom one could cover the door of Soo's room and the space in front of the window arch, the part of the room beyond, where the couch stood, was out of range.

'How did Meng explain his presence in the armoury?' Dee asked the Commander. 'He said clearly that he wouldn't go up there that day, didn't he?'

Fang nodded unhappily. 'The idiot said that after he had gone up to his room to lie down, he found there a note from Soo, ordering him to meet him in the armoury at two. When asked to produce the note, he said he had thrown it away! We considered that story as strong proof of Meng's guilt.'

'It does indeed look bad for him,' Judge Dee agreed. 'Meng didn't know that Kao would go up to the leather room. If Kao hadn't surprised him, he would have sneaked back to his own room after the deed, and no one would have suspected him.' He stepped up to the desk and picked up the arrow lying next to the iron helmet. It was about four foot long, and much heavier than he expected. Its long, needle-sharp iron point, provided at the base with two wicked barbs, showed some brownish spots. 'I suppose this was the arrow that killed Soo?'

The Commander nodded. 'We had a messy job getting it out,' he remarked, 'because of the barbs.'

Judge Dee examined the arrow carefully. The shaft was lacquered red, with black feathers attached to the end. Just below the iron point, the shaft had been reinforced by red tape tightly wound around it.

'Nothing special about the arrow,' Mao said impatiently. 'Regular army issue.'

'I see that the red tape is torn,' Judge Dee remarked. 'There is a jagged tear, parallel with the shaft.'

The others made no comment. The judge's remarks didn't seem to strike them as very brilliant. He didn't think much of them himself, either. With a sigh he put the arrow back on the desk and said:

'I must admit there's a strong case against Colonel Meng. He had the motive, the opportunity, and the particular skill required to utilize the opportunity. I'll have to think this over. Before leaving the fort, though, I'd like to see Colonel Meng. Perhaps Lieutenant Kao could take me to him, then I'll have seen all persons concerned in this vexing affair.'

The Commander gave the judge a searching look. He seemed to hesitate, then he barked an order at Colonel Mao.

While Lieutenant Kao was conducting him to the prison at the rear of the fort, Judge Dee unobtrusively studied his companion. Kao was a good-looking youngster, very trim in his close-fitting mail coat and round helmet. The judge tried to make him talk about the murder, but got only very curt answers. The young man was either overawed or extremely nervous.

A giant of a man was pacing the cell, his hands behind his back. As he saw the two men arrive in front of the heavy iron bars, his face lit up and he said in a deep voice: 'Good to see you, Kao! Any news?'

'The magistrate is here, sir,' Kao said rather diffidently. 'He wants to ask you a few questions.'

Judge Dee told Kao that he could leave. Then he addressed the prisoner:

'Commander Fang told me that the court martial pronounced you guilty of premeditated murder. If there is anything you might adduce for a plea for clemency, I should be glad to help you formulate that plea. My two lieutenants Ma and Chiao spoke highly of you.'

'I didn't murder Soo, sir,' the giant said gruffly. 'But they found me guilty, so let them chop my head off. That's the army statute, and a man has to die sooner or later anyway. There's no occasion for any plea.'

'If you are innocent,' the judge resumed, 'it means that the murderer must have had a compelling reason for wanting both Soo and you out of the way. For it was he who sent you the faked note, to make you the scapegoat. So that narrows down the number of suspects. Can you think of anybody who had reason to hate both you and Vice-Commander Soo?'

'There were too many who hated Soo. He was a good administrator but a real martinet; he had the men flogged at the slightest provocation. As for me, well, I always thought I had only friends here. If I offended someone, I did it unwittingly. So that doesn't help very much.'

Judge Dee silently agreed. He thought for a while, then resumed, 'Tell me exactly what you did after you came back to the fort, the night before the murder.'

'The morning, rather!' Meng said with a wry smile. 'It was long after midnight, you know! The boat trip back had sobered me up a bit, but I was still in a happy mood. The captain of the guard, a good fellow, helped me to get up to my room. I made a bit of a nuisance of myself, and wouldn't let him go, insisting on telling him in considerable detail about the good time we'd had, what nice fellows those two Koreans were, and about their splendid hospitality. Pak and Yee their names were—funny pronunciation those people have!' He scratched his unruly head, then went on, 'Yes, I remember that I let the captain go only after he had solemnly promised me that he would come along too, next week. I had told him that Pak and Yee had said they'd have even more money to spend then, and were determined to throw a real party for me and all my friends. I laid myself down on my bed fully dressed, feeling perfectly happy. But the next morning I didn't feel happy any more! I had the father and mother of all headaches. Somehow or other I managed to get through the morning drill, but I was glad when it was over and I could go up to my room for a nap. Then, just as I was going to throw myself on my bed, I saw that note. I . . .'

'Couldn't you see it was faked?' the judge interrupted.

'Heavens no, I am no student of calligraphy! Besides, it was just a few scrawled words. But Soo's seal was on it and that was genuine—I have seen it a hundred times on all sorts of papers. If the seal hadn't been on it, I would have thought it a prank by a colleague and would have checked with Soo. But that seal made it genuine all right, and I went up to the armoury at once. Soo didn't relish people questioning his orders! And that's how my trouble started!'

'You didn't look out of the window while you were in the armoury?'

'Why should I? I expected Soo to come up at any moment. I examined a couple of crossbows, that's all.'

31

'YOU ARE SHIELDING SOMEONE, MENG!' JUDGE DEE SAID ANGRILY

Judge Dee studied Meng's broad honest face. Suddenly he stepped up to the bars and shouted angrily:

'You are shielding someone, Meng!'

Meng grew red in the face. Gripping the bars with his large powerful hands, he growled, 'You are talking nonsense! You are a civilian. You'd better not meddle in military affairs!' He turned round and resumed his pacing.

'Have it your own way!' Judge Dee said coldly. He walked down the corridor. The turnkey opened the heavy iron door, and Lieutenant Kao took him to the Commander's office.

'Well, what do you think of Meng?' Fang asked.

'I admit he doesn't seem the type that murders a man in his sleep,' Judge Dee replied cautiously. 'But one never knows, of course. By the way, I have mislaid one of the copies of the official correspondence you always let me have so kindly. Could I have an extra copy, just to complete my file? The number of the document is P-404.'

The Commander looked astonished at this unexpected request, but he ordered his aide to get the paper from the archives.

The officer was back in a remarkably short time. He handed the Commander two sheets. Fang glanced them through, then gave them to the judge, saying, 'Here you are! Routine matter.'

Judge Dee saw that the first page contained a proposal that Kao and three other lieutenants be promoted to the rank of captain, together with a list of their names, ages and terms of service. It was stamped with the impression of Soo's seal. The second sheet contained only a few lines, wherein the Commander expressed the hope that the Board of Military Affairs would speedily approve his proposal. It bore the Commander's large seal, the date and the number P-404.

The Judge shook his head. 'There must be a mistake somewhere. The missing paper must have dealt with the purchase of material, for the next number, P-405, a request for the supply of leather belts, refers back to P-404. Therefore P in P-404 must stand for Purchases, and not for Personnel.'

'Holy heaven!' the Commander exclaimed, 'clerks do make mistakes sometimes, don't they? Well, thanks very much for

33

your visit, Magistrate. Let me know when you have formulated your opinion on Soo's murder.'

While the judge was stepping outside he vaguely heard the Commander muttering something to his aide about 'silly red tape'.

The fiery midday sun had transformed the quay in front of the gate into a brick oven, but as soon as the barge was well out into the river, there was an agreeably cool breeze. The sergeant in charge of the barge had seen to it that the judge and his two lieutenants had comfortable seats on the platform at the stern, under an awning of green cloth.

As soon as the orderly, who had brought a large teapot, had disappeared into the hold, Ma Joong and Chiao Tai stormed the judge with questions.

'I really don't know what to think,' Judge Dee said slowly. 'All appearances are against Meng, but I have a vague suspicion that the fool is shielding someone. Did you two learn anything?'

Ma Joong and Chiao Tai shook their heads. The latter said:

'We had a long talk with the captain of the guard who was on duty when Meng came back to the fort after his spree with us. He likes Meng, the same as everybody else in the fort. He didn't mind practically carrying Meng up to his room, though that was by no means an easy job! And Meng kept on singing bawdy songs at the top of his voice. He must have wakened up all his colleagues, I fear! The captain said also that Meng was no special friend of Soo's, but that Meng respected him as an able officer, and didn't take Soo's frequent fits of anger too seriously.'

Judge Dee made no comment. He remained silent for a long time. Sipping his tea, he looked at the peaceful scenery floating by. Both banks were lined with green rice fields, dotted here and there with the yellow straw hats of the farmers working there. Suddenly he said, 'Colonel Shih Lang also thinks that Meng is innocent. But Colonel Mao, the chief of the military police, believes he's guilty.'

'Meng often told us about Shih Lang,' Ma Joong said. 'Meng is the champion archer, but Shih Lang is the champion at scaling walls! The fellow is one bunch of muscle! He is in charge of drilling the soldiers in this art. They strip down to their under-clothes, and with bare feet they have to tackle an old wall. They learn to use their toes as if they were fingers. When they have found a hold, they work their toes into a crack below, then reach up to find a higher hold, repeating this till they get to the top of the wall. I'd like to try it myself some day! As for that Colonel Mao, he is a nasty suspicious specimen; everybody is agreed on that!'

Judge Dee nodded. 'According to Meng, the two Koreans footed the bill for your party.'

'Oh,' Chiao Tai said a little self-consciously, 'that was because of a rather silly prank we played on them! We were in a gay mood, and when Pak asked us about our professions, we said all three of us were highwaymen. The two fellows believed us; they said they might have work for us some day! When we wanted to pay our share, it turned out that they had settled the whole bill already.'

'But we are going to meet them again next week when they are back from the capital,' Ma Joong said. 'Then we'll tell them the truth and the evening'll be on us. We hate sponging.'

'It may disappoint them,' Chiao Tai added, 'for Pak and Yee are expecting payment for three junks, and they are all set on having a big celebration then. Did you get the joke about those three boats by the way, Brother Ma? After Pak and Yee had told us about that business deal, both of them got such a fit of laughter that they nearly rolled under the table!'

'That's where I nearly landed too!' Ma Joong said ruefully.

The judge had not heard the last remark, he was deep in thought, slowly stroking his black beard. Suddenly he said to Ma Joong, 'Tell me more about that night! Especially how Meng acted, and what he said.'

'Well,' Ma Joong replied, 'Brother Chiao and I go to the crab restaurant on the quay, it's nice and cool there. About dinner time we see the military barge come alongside, and Meng and another fellow get out. They say good-bye, then Meng comes strolling over to us on the terrace. He says he has had rather a heavy day at the fort, so we should have a really good meal. And that's what we did. Then . . .'

'Did Meng say anything about the Vice-Commander, or about Lieutenant Kao?' the judge interrupted him.

'Not a word!'

'Did he seem to have anything on his mind?'

'Nothing beyond a base desire for a nice girl!' Ma Joong replied with a grin. 'Accordingly we go to the flowerboats, and there Meng gets that particular problem off his mind. While we are having a few rounds on deck, those two fellows Pak and Yee arrive in a boat, drunk as can be. The madame can't get them interested in business, although she trots out the best she has. The only thing Pak and Yee want is more wine, and lots of it, and some congenial conversation. So the five of us start on a protracted drinking bout. I am not clear about the rest—Brother Chiao had better take up the story from there!'

'You disappeared from sight, let's leave it at that,' Chiao Tai said dryly. 'As for me, a couple of hours after midnight I helped Meng lower the two Koreans into a rowboat, to be taken back to the Korean quarter on the other side of the canal. Then Meng and I whistled for another boat, and had ourselves rowed to the quay. When I had put Meng on the military barge waiting there, I felt rather tired, and since the crab restaurant was so near, I asked them to put me up for the night. That's all.'

'I see,' said Judge Dee.

He drank a few more cups of tea, then he suddenly set his cup down and asked, 'Where are we here?'

Ma Joong looked at the river bank, then answered, 'About half-way to Peng-lai, I'd say.'

'Tell the sergeant to turn the barge round and take us back to the fort,' the judge ordered.

Ma Joong and Chiao Tai tried to elicit from the judge the reason for his sudden decision, but he only said he wanted to verify two or three points he had overlooked.

Back at the fort an aide-de-camp informed them that the Commander was in a secret staff conference, discussing important intelligence reports that had just come in.

'Don't disturb him!' Judge Dee told him. 'Get me Colonel Mao!'

He explained to the astonished chief of the military police that he wanted to have another look at the scene of the murder, and that he wished him to be present, as a witness.

Looking more cynical than ever, Colonel Mao led the three men upstairs. He broke the paper strip that had again been pasted over the lock on the door of Soo's room, and bade the judge enter.

Before stepping inside, Judge Dee told Ma Joong and Chiao Tai, 'I am looking for something small and sharp, say a splinter, or the head of a nail, and roughly within this area.' He indicated a square space of the floor, beginning at the door and ending halfway across the room in front of the window arch. Then he squatted down and began to examine the floorboards inch by inch. His two lieutenants joined him.

'If you are looking for a secret trap-door or any such hocus-pocus,' Colonel Mao said with heavy irony, 'I must disappoint you. This fort was built only a few years ago, you know!'

'Here—I have something!' Ma Joong exclaimed. He pointed at a spot in front of the window where the sharp edge of the head of a nail protruded from the floorboard.

'Excellent!' the judge exclaimed. He knelt down and scrutinized the nail-head. Then he got up and asked Mao, 'Would you mind prying loose that tiny fragment of red material sticking to the head of the nail? And at the same time have a good look at those small brownish spots on the wood there!'

Mao straightened himself, looking doubtfully at the small piece of red tape on his thumbnail.

'In due time,' Judge Dee said gravely, 'I shall ask you to testify that the fragment of red tape was indeed found stuck to the head of the nail. Also, that the brown spots found near it are most probably traces of human blood.' Ignoring the Colonel's excited questions, Judge Dee took the arrow from the desk and drove it into the floorboard next to the nail-head. 'This'll mark the exact spot!' He thought for a while, then asked, 'What happened to the dead man's personal effects, and to the contents of that desk drawer?'

Irritated by Judge Dee's peremptory tone, Mao replied coldly: 'Those objects were collected in two separate containers, which I asked the Commander to seal. They are locked away in my

37

office. We of the military police are, of course, not as clever and experienced as officers of the tribunal, but we know our job, I trust!'

'All right, all right!' the judge said impatiently. 'Take us to your office!'

Colonel Mao asked Judge Dee to sit down at his large desk, which was littered with papers. Ma Joong and Chiao Tai remained standing by the door. Mao unlocked an iron chest and took from it two packages wrapped up in oiled paper. Placing one in front of the judge, he said:

'This is what we found in the leather folder the Vice-Commander carried on a string round his neck, under his mail jacket.'

Judge Dee broke the seal and arranged on the desk a folded identification card of the Imperial Army, a receipted bill for the purchase of a house dated seven years before, and a small square brocade carrying-case for a personal seal. He opened the latter, and seemed pleased when it proved to be empty. 'I presume,' he said to Mao, 'that the seal itself was found in the drawer of the dead man's desk?'

'It was. It's in the second package, together with the papers we found in the drawer. I thought it rather careless of Soo to let his personal seal lie about in that unlocked drawer. As a rule people always carry their seal on their person.'

'They do indeed,' Judge Dee said. He rose and added, 'I don't need to inspect the other package. Let's go and see whether the Commander is through with his conference.'

The two sentries who stood guard outside the door of the council room informed them that the conference had just ended and that tea would soon be brought in. Judge Dee brushed past them without more ado.

Commander Fang was seated at the main table in the centre of the room. At the side table on his left sat Colonel Shih Lang, and another officer the judge did not know. At the table on the other side two senior officers were sitting, and Lieutenant Kao was sorting out a pile of papers on a small table apart; evidently he had been taking notes of the proceedings. All rose from their chairs when they saw the judge enter.

'Please excuse this intrusion,' Judge Dee said calmly as he advanced to the Commander's table. 'I came to report my findings regarding the murder of Vice-Commander Soo. Am I right in assuming that the officers assembled here form the quorum for a court martial?'

'If you include Colonel Mao over there, they do,' Fang replied slowly.

'Excellent! Please let Colonel Meng be brought in, so that we can have a regular session of the court martial.'

The Commander gave an order to his aide, then he pulled a chair up to his table and invited Judge Dee to sit down by his side. Ma Joong and Chiao Tai went to stand behind their master's chair.

Two orderlies came in with trays. All drank their tea in silence.

Then the door opened again. Four military police in full armour came in with Colonel Meng in their midst. Meng stepped up to the central table and saluted smartly.

The Commander cleared his throat. 'We are convened today to hear a report by Magistrate Dee, drawn up at my request, and to decide whether the said report shall necessitate a review of the case against Colonel Meng Kwo-tai, convicted of the premeditated murder of Soo, Vice-Commander of this fort. I request Magistrate Dee to make his report.'

'The motive for this murder,' Judge Dee began in an even voice, 'was to prevent the Vice-Commander from starting an investigation of a clever fraud, by which a criminal hoped to acquire a large amount of money.

'I must remind you of the office routine regarding requests for the purchase of military supplies needed for this fort. After a request has been drafted by the Commander in council, a clerk writes the text out on official paper and it is passed on to the Vice-Commander, who checks its contents and impresses his seal on every page. He then gives the document to the Commander who rechecks it and impresses his seal at the end. When the customary number of copies have been made, the original is put in an envelope addressed to the Board of Military Affairs in the capital, sealed and forwarded there by despatch riders.'

Judge Dee took a sip of his tea, then went on, 'This system has

39

only one loophole. If the document consists of more than one sheet, a dishonest person here who has access to the official correspondence may destroy all sheets but the last one that bears the Commander's seal, substitute spurious ones and then send the document to the capital, including the authentic last page.'

'Impossible!' Commander Fang interrupted. 'The other sheets must bear the seal of the Vice-Commander!'

'That's why he was murdered!' the judge said. 'The criminal purloined Soo's seal, and Soo discovered it. However, before going further into that, I'll first explain how the laudable devotion to office routine of a clerk here put me on the criminal's track.

'Three days ago, a request for the promotion of four lieutenants offered the criminal his chance. The proposal, as written out in its final form, consisted of two sheets. The first contained the request together with the names, ages, etc. of the four persons concerned. The second sheet contained only the Commander's recommendation for speedy action (in general terms, mind you!), the date and the file number: P for Personnel and the figure 404. The first page bore Soo's seal, the second that of the Commander.

'The criminal got hold of this paper on its way to the despatch section. He destroyed the first sheet and replaced it by one on which he had written an urgent request for the purchase of three war junks from the Korean merchants Pak and Yee, adding that the Board of Military Affairs was to pay out the purchase price— a small fortune!—to the said two merchants. After the criminal had marked this spurious page with Soo's purloined seal, he himself put it in an envelope and addressed it: Board of Military Affairs, Section of Supplies. Finally he wrote in a corner of the envelope the number of the paper it contained, namely P-404, as prescribed. He gave the closed envelope to the despatch clerk; the extra copies of the original letter containing the request for the promotion of the four lieutenants he himself entered into the archives. Since he was not familiar with the new rules for distribution, he omitted to have one of those copies sent to my tribunal.

'Now it so happened that the same despatch clerk who sent out the sealed envelope marked P-404 received that same day another letter numbered P-405 containing a request for the purchase of leather goods. He remembered that the two Ps for Purchase and

Personnel sometimes gave rise to confusion in the archives. Therefore, being a good bureaucrat, he added to this number P-405 a note saying, "Refer back to P-404"; for although he had not seen the paper P-404, he remembered that the Section of Supplies had been mentioned on the envelope. The clerk distributed the copies of P-405 correctly, including one extra copy for me. But when I checked my Purchases file, I found P-404 missing. That annoyed me, for I believe in keeping my files complete. Therefore I asked the Commander here to let me have an extra copy. He gave me a letter concerning the promotion of four lieutenants, which belonged therefore to Personnel.'

The Commander, who had been shifting impatiently on his chair, now burst out: 'Couldn't you skip all these details? What is all that nonsense about three war junks?'

'The criminal,' Judge Dee replied calmly, 'was in collusion with the merchants Pak and Yee. Having received in the capital the money for this imaginary purchase, they were going to share it with the criminal. Since it would be many weeks before the routine checks in the Board of Military Affairs revealed the discrepancy with your reports on supplies received, the criminal had plenty of time to prepare his abscondence with the money.

'It was a clever scheme, but he had bad luck. On the night preceding the murder, Colonel Meng and my two assistants met the two Korean merchants in the city and they got drunk together. The merchants thought the three men were highway robbers, and said something about the junks and the money they were going to get for them in the capital. My assistants reported that to me, and I put two and two together. I may add that when Meng came back to the fort he boasted to the captain of the guard about the munificence of Pak and Yee, and that there was more to come. The murderer overheard this and concluded—wrongly—that Meng knew too much, which fortified him in his plan to make Meng the scapegoat. When the criminal learned the next morning that Meng had a hangover and had decided not to go up to the armoury, he sent him a faked message, sealing it with Soo's seal which he still had in his possession.'

'I don't follow all this!' the Commander exclaimed crossly. 'What I want to know is: who shot Soo, and how?'

'Fair enough!' the judge said. 'Colonel Shih Lang murdered Soo.'

It was very still. Then the Commander spoke angrily:

'Utterly impossible! Lieutenant Kao saw Colonel Shih Lang enter and leave Soo's room; Shih Lang didn't even go near Soo's couch!'

Judge Dee continued calmly, 'Colonel Shih Lang went up to Soo's room a little before two, directly after wall-scaling drill. That means that he was clad only in an undergarment, and was barefoot. He couldn't take any weapon, and he didn't need to. For he knew that Soo was in the habit of throwing his quiver into the window recess, and his plan was to grab an arrow and stab Soo to death in his sleep.

'However, when Shih Lang came in he saw that Soo had got up. He had stepped into his boots and was standing in front of his couch, wearing his mail jacket. Thus Shih Lang couldn't stab him as planned. But then the murderer saw that one arrow had dropped out of the quiver and lay on the floor pointing at Soo. Shih Lang stepped on it, put his big toe and the next around the shaft directly behind the point, and with a powerful kick sent it flying into Soo's unprotected abdomen. At the same time he put on an act for Meng, in case he was looking out of the armoury window: he waved his arms and started to shout—drowning the cries of his victim as he fell backwards on the couch. When he had made sure his victim was dead, he went outside and called the guards. Then, having come back to the room together with the Commander and Colonel Mao, he slipped Soo's seal into the drawer of the desk during the general confusion. It was neatly done; he overlooked only one fact, namely that the dead man would be found with his boots on. That suggested to me that Soo had not been killed in his sleep. It was understandable that Soo should have kept his mail jacket on while taking a brief nap, for it's quite a job to get it off. But he had thrown his helmet on the desk, and one would have expected him also to have stepped out of his boots before lying down.'

The judge paused. All eyes were now on Colonel Shih Lang. He gave Judge Dee a contemptuous look and asked with a sneer: 'And how do you propose to prove this fantastic theory?'

42

'For the time being,' the judge replied calmly, 'by the fact that you have a nasty scratch on the big toe of your right foot. For where the arrow was lying, the sharp edge of a nail head protruded from the floorboards. It tore the red tape round the arrow's shaft when you kicked it up, and also scratched your toe. Small bloodstains mark the spot. The final proof will be here later, when Pak and Yee have been arrested, and the false document traced in the Board of Military Affairs.'

Shih Lang's face had become livid, his lips were twitching. But he pulled himself together and said in a steady voice, 'You needn't wait for that. I murdered Soo. I am in debt and needed the money. In ten days I'd have applied for sick leave, and never come back. It hadn't been my intention to kill Soo. I had hoped to be able to return the seal by leaving it on his desk. But he discovered the loss too soon, so I decided to stab him with an arrow while he was asleep. But when I came in I saw that Soo was up and about. He shouted at me: "Now I have verified my suspicions, it was you who stole my seal!" I thought I was lost, for tackling Soo armed only with an arrow would be a difficult proposition, and if Meng looked out of the window he would see our struggle. Then my eye fell on the arrow on the floor, and I kicked it up into Soo's guts.' He wiped the perspiration from his brow and concluded: 'I am not sorry, for Soo was a mean bastard. I regret that I had to make you the scapegoat, Meng, but it couldn't be helped. That's all!'

The Commander rose from his chair. 'Your sword, Shih Lang!'

As the colonel unbuckled his swordbelt he said bitterly to the judge: 'You sly devil! How did you get on to me?'

Judge Dee replied primly: 'Mainly by red tape!'

HE CAME WITH THE RAIN

The scene of this third story is also laid in Peng-lai about half a year later. In the meantime Judge Dee's two wives and their children arrived in Peng-lai, and settled down in the magistrate's private residence at the back of the tribunal compound. Shortly afterwards, Miss Tsao joined the household. In Chapter XV of The Chinese Gold Murders the terrible adventure from which Judge Dee extricated Miss Tsao has been described in detail. When Judge Dee's First Lady met Miss Tsao, she took an instant liking to her and engaged her as her lady-companion. Then, on one of the hottest, rainy days of mid-summer, there occurred the strange case related in the present story.

'This box won't do either!' Judge Dee's First Lady remarked disgustedly. 'Look at the grey mould all along the seam of this blue dress!' She slammed the lid of the red-leather clothes-box shut, then turned to the Second Lady. 'I've never known such a hot, damp summer. And the heavy downpour we had last night! I thought the rain would never stop. Give me a hand, will you?'

The judge, seated at the tea-table by the open window of the large bedroom, looked on while his two wives put the clothes-box on the floor, and went on to the third one in the pile. Miss Tsao, his First Lady's friend and companion, was drying robes on the brass brazier in the corner, draping them over the copper-wire cover above the glowing coals. The heat of the brazier, together with the steam curling up from the drying clothes, made the atmosphere of the room nearly unbearable, but the three women seemed unaware of it.

With a sigh he turned round and looked outside. From the bedroom here on the second floor of his residence one usually had a fine view of the curved roofs of the city, but now everything was shrouded in a thick leaden mist that blotted out all contours. The mist seemed to have entered his very blood, pulsating dully in his veins. Now he deeply regretted the unfortunate impulse that, on rising, had made him ask for his grey summer robe. For that request had brought his First Lady to inspect the four clothes-boxes, and finding mould on the garments, she had at once summoned his Second and Miss Tsao. Now the three were completely engrossed in their work, with apparently no thought of morning tea, let alone breakfast. This was their first experience of the dog-days in Peng-lai, for it was just seven months since he had taken up his post of magistrate there. He stretched his legs, for his knees and feet felt swollen and heavy. Miss Tsao stooped and took a white dress from the brazier.

'This one is completely dry,' she announced. As she reached up to hang it on the clothes-rack, the judge noticed her slender, shapely body. Suddenly he asked his First Lady sharply: 'Can't you leave all that to the maids?'

'Of course,' his First replied over her shoulder. 'But first I want to see for myself whether there's any real damage. For heaven's sake, take a look at this red robe, dear!' she went on to Miss Tsao. 'The mould has absolutely eaten into the fabric! And you always say this dress looks so well on me!'

Judge Dee rose abruptly. The smell of perfume and stale cosmetics mingling with the faint odour of damp clothes gave the hot room an atmosphere of overwhelming femininity that suddenly jarred on his taut nerves. 'I'm just going out for a short walk,' he said.

'Before you've even had your morning tea?' his First exclaimed. But her eyes were on the discoloured patches on the red dress in her hands.

'I'll be back for breakfast,' the judge muttered. 'Give me that blue robe over there!' Miss Tsao helped the Second put the robe over his shoulders and asked solicitously: 'Isn't that dress a bit too heavy for this hot weather?'

'It's dry at least,' he said curtly. At the same time he realized with dismay that Miss Tsao was perfectly right: the thick fabric clung to his moist back like a coat of mail. He mumbled a greeting and went downstairs.

He quickly walked down the semi-dark corridor leading to the small back door of the tribunal compound. He was glad his old friend and adviser Sergeant Hoong had not yet appeared. The sergeant knew him so well that he would sense at once that he was in a bad temper, and he would wonder what it was all about.

The judge opened the back door with his private key and slipped out into the wet, deserted street. What was it all about, really? he asked himself as he walked along through the dripping mist. Well, these seven months on his first independent official post had been disappointing, of course. The first few days had been exciting, and then there had been the murder of Mrs Ho, and the case at the fort. But thereafter there had been nothing but dreary office routine: forms to be filled out, papers to be filed, licences to be issued. . . . In the capital he had also had much paperwork to do, but on important papers. Moreover, this district was not really his. The entire region from the river north was a strategic area, under the jurisdiction of the army. And the Korean quarter outside the East Gate had its own administration. He angrily kicked a stone, then cursed. What had looked like a loose boulder was in fact the top of a cobblestone, and he hurt his toe badly. He must take a decision about Miss Tsao. The night before, in the intimacy of their shared couch, his First Lady had again urged him to take Miss Tsao as his Third. She and his Second were fond of her, she had said, and Miss Tsao herself wanted nothing better. 'Besides,' his First had added with her customary frankness, 'your Second is a fine woman but she hasn't had a higher education, and to have an intelligent, well-read girl like Miss Tsao around would make life much more interesting for all concerned.' But what if Miss Tsao's willingness was motivated only by gratitude to him for getting her out of the terrible trouble she had been in? In a way it would be easier if he didn't like her so much. On the other hand, would it then be fair to marry a woman one didn't really like? As a magistrate he was entitled to as many as four wives, but personally he held the view that two wives ought to be sufficient unless both of them proved barren. It was all very difficult and confusing. He pulled his robe closer round him, for it had begun to rain.

He sighed with relief when he saw the broad steps leading up to the Temple of Confucius. The third floor of the west tower had been converted into a small tea-house. He would have his morning tea there, then walk back to the tribunal.

In the low-ceilinged, octagonal room a slovenly dressed waiter was leaning on the counter, stirring the fire of the small tea-stove with iron tongs. Judge Dee noticed with satisfaction that the youngster didn't recognize him, for he was not in the mood to acknowledge bowing and scraping. He ordered a pot of tea and a dry towel and sat down at the bamboo table in front of the the counter.

The waiter handed him a none-too-clean towel in a bamboo basket. 'Just one moment please, sir. The water'll be boiling soon.' As the judge rubbed his long beard dry with the towel, the waiter went on, 'Since you are up and about so early, sir, you'll have heard already about the trouble out there.' He pointed with his thumb at the open window, and as the judge shook his head, he continued with relish, 'Last night a fellow was hacked to pieces in the old watchtower, out there in the marsh.'

Judge Dee quickly put the towel down. 'A murder? How do you know?'

'The grocery boy told me, sir. Came up here to deliver his stuff while I was scrubbing the floor. At dawn he had gone to that watchtower to collect duck eggs from that half-witted girl who lives up there, and he saw the mess. The girl was sitting crying in a corner. Rushing back to town, he warned the military police at the blockhouse, and the captain went to the old tower with a few of his men. Look, there they are!'

Judge Dee got up and went to the window. From this vantage-point he could see beyond the crenellated top of the city wall the vast green expanse of the marshlands overgrown with reeds, and further on to the north, in the misty distance, the grey water of the river. A hardened road went from the quay north of the city straight to the lonely tower of weather-beaten bricks in the middle of the marsh. A few soldiers with spiked helmets came marching down the road to the blockhouse halfway between the tower and the quay.

'Was the murdered man a soldier?' the judge asked quickly. Although the area north of the city came under the jurisdiction of the army, any crime involving civilians there had to be referred to the tribunal.

'Could be. That half-witted girl is deaf and dumb, but not too bad-looking. Could be a soldier went up the tower for a private

47

conversation with her, if you get what I mean. Ha, the water is boiling!'

Judge Dee strained his eyes. Now two military policemen were riding from the blockhouse to the city, their horses splashing through the water that had submerged part of the raised road.

'Here's your tea, sir! Be careful, the cup is very hot. I'll put it here on the sill for you. No, come to think of it, the murdered man was no soldier. The grocery boy said he was an old merchant living near the North Gate—he knew him by sight. Well, the military police will catch the murderer soon enough. Plenty tough, they are!' He nudged the judge excitedly. 'There you are! Didn't I tell you they're tough? See that fellow in chains they're dragging from the blockhouse? He's wearing a fisherman's brown jacket and trousers. Well, they'll take him to the fort now, and . . .'

'They'll do nothing of the sort!' the judge interrupted angrily. He hastily took a sip from the tea and scalded his mouth. He paid and rushed downstairs. A civilian murdered by another civilian, that was clearly a case for the tribunal! This was a splendid occasion to tell the military exactly where they got off! Once and for all.

All his apathy had dropped away from him. He rented a horse from the blacksmith on the corner, jumped into the saddle and rode to the North Gate. The guards cast an astonished look at the dishevelled horseman with the wet house-cap sagging on his head. But then they recognized their magistrate and sprang to attention. The judge dismounted and motioned the corporal to follow him into the guardhouse beside the gate. 'What is all this commotion out on the marsh?' he asked.

'A man was found murdered in the old tower, sir. The military police have arrested the murderer already; they are questioning him now in the blockhouse. I expect they'll come down to the quay presently.'

Judge Dee sat down on the bamboo bench and handed the corporal a few coppers. 'Tell one of your men to buy me two oilcakes!'

The oilcakes came fresh from the griddle of a street vendor and had an appetizing smell of garlic and onions, but the judge did not enjoy them, hungry though he was. The hot tea had burnt his tongue, and his mind was concerned with the abuse of power by the army authorities. He reflected ruefully that in the capital one didn't have such annoying problems to cope with : there, detailed rules fixed the exact extent of the authority of every official, high or low. As he was finishing his oilcakes, the corporal came in.

'The military police have now taken the prisoner to their watch-post on the quay, sir.'

Judge Dee sprang up. 'Follow me with four men !'

On the river quay a slight breeze was dispersing the mist. The judge's robe clung wetly to his shoulders. 'Exactly the kind of weather for catching a bad cold,' he muttered. A heavily armed sentry ushered him into the bare waiting-room of the watchpost.

In the back a tall man wearing the coat of mail and spiked helmet of the military police was sitting behind a roughly made wooden desk. He was filling out an official form with laborious, slow strokes of his writing-brush.

'I am Magistrate Dee,' the judge began. 'I demand to know . . .' He suddenly broke off. The captain had looked up. His face was marked by a terrible white scar running along his left cheek and across his mouth. His misshapen lips were half-concealed by a ragged moustache. Before the judge had recovered from this shock, the captain had risen. He saluted smartly and said in a clipped voice :

'Glad you came, sir. I have just finished my report to you.' Pointing at the stretcher covered with a blanket on the floor in the corner, he added, 'That's the dead body, and the murderer is in the back room there. You want him taken directly to the jail of the tribunal, I suppose?'

'Yes. Certainly,' Judge Dee replied, rather lamely.

'Good.' The captain folded the sheet he had been writing on and handed it to the judge. 'Sit down, sir. If you have a moment to spare, I'd like to tell you myself about the case.'

Judge Dee took the seat by the desk and motioned the captain to sit down too. Stroking his long beard, he said to himself that all this was turning out quite differently from what he had expected.

'Well,' the captain began, 'I know the marshland as well as the palm of my hand. That deaf-mute girl who lives in the tower is a harmless idiot, so when it was reported that a murdered man was lying up in her room, I thought at once of assault and robbery, and sent my men to search the marshland between the tower and the riverbank.'

'Why especially that area?' the judge interrupted. 'It could just as well have happened on the road, couldn't it? The murderer hiding the dead body later in the tower?'

'No, sir. Our blockhouse is located on the road halfway between the quay here and the old tower. From there my men keep an eye on the road all day long, as per orders. To prevent Korean spies from entering or leaving the city, you see. And they patrol that road at night. That road is the only means of crossing the marsh, by the way. It's tricky country, and anyone trying to cross it would risk getting into a swamp or quicksand and would drown. Now my men found the body was still warm, and we concluded he was killed a few hours before dawn. Since no one passed the blockhouse except the grocery boy, it follows that both the murdered man and the criminal came from the north. A pathway leads through the reeds from the tower to the riverbank, and a fellow familiar with the layout could slip by there without my men in the blockhouse spotting him.' The captain stroked his moustache and added, 'If he had succeeded in getting by our river patrols, that is.'

'And your men caught the murderer by the waterside?'

'Yes, sir. They discovered a young fisherman, Wang San-lang his name is, hiding in his small boat among the rushes, directly north of the tower. He was trying to wash his trousers which were stained with blood. When my men hailed him, he pushed off and tried to paddle his boat into midstream. The archers shot a few string arrows into the hull, and before he knew where he was he was being hauled back to shore, boat and all. He disclaimed all knowledge of any dead man in the tower, maintained he was on his way there to bring the deaf-mute girl a large carp, and that he got the blood on his trousers while cleaning that carp. He was waiting for dawn to visit her. We searched him, and we found this in his belt.'

The captain unwrapped a small paper package on his desk and showed the judge three shining silver pieces. 'We identified the corpse by the visiting-cards we found on it.' He shook the contents of a large envelope out on the table. Besides a package of cards there were two keys, some small change, and a pawn-ticket. Pointing at the ticket, the captain continued, 'That scrap of paper was lying on the floor, close to the body. Must have dropped out of his jacket. The murdered man is the pawnbroker Choong, the owner of a large and well-known pawnshop, just inside the North Gate. A wealthy man. His hobby is fishing. My theory is that Choong met Wang somewhere on the quay last night and hired him to take him out in his boat for a night of fishing on the river. When they had got to the deserted area north of the tower, Wang lured the old man there under some pretext or other and killed him. He had planned to hide the body somewhere in the tower—the thing is half in ruins, you know, and the girl uses only the second storey—but she woke up and caught him in the act. So he just took the silver and left. This is only a theory, mind you, for the girl is worthless as a witness. My men tried to get something out of her, but she only scribbled down some incoherent nonsense about rain spirits and black goblins. Then she had a fit, began to laugh and to cry at the same time. A poor, harmless half-wit.' He rose, walked over to the stretcher and lifted the blanket. 'Here's the dead body.'

Judge Dee bent over the lean shape, which was clad in a simple brown robe. The breast showed patches of clotted blood, and the sleeves were covered with dried mud. The face had a peaceful look, but it was very ugly: lantern-shaped, with a beaked nose that was slightly askew, and a thin-lipped, too large mouth. The head with its long, greying hair was bare.

'Not a very handsome gentleman,' the captain remarked. 'Though I should be the last to pass such a remark!' A spasm contorted his mutilated face. He raised the body's shoulders and showed the judge the large red stain on the back. 'Killed by a knife thrust from behind that must have penetrated right into his heart. He was lying on his back on the floor, just inside the door of the girl's room.' The captain let the upper part of the body drop. 'Nasty fellow, that fisherman. After he had murdered

51

Choong, he began to cut up his breast and belly. I say *after* he had killed him, for as you see those wounds in front haven't bled as much as one would expect. Oh yes, here's my last exhibit! Had nearly forgotten it!' He pulled out a drawer in the desk and unwrapped the oiled paper of an oblong package. Handing the judge a long thin knife, he said, 'This was found in Wang's boat, sir. He says he uses it for cleaning his fish. There was no trace of blood on it. Why should there be? There was plenty of water around to wash it clean after he had got back to the boat! Well, that's about all, sir. I expect that Wang'll confess readily enough. I know that type of young hoodlum. They begin by stoutly denying everything, but after a thorough interrogation they break down and then they talk their mouths off. What are your orders, sir?'

'First I must inform the next of kin, and have them formally identify the body. Therefore, I . . .'

'I've attended to that, sir. Choong was a widower, and his two sons are living in the capital. The body was officially identified just now by Mr Lin, the dead man's partner, who lived together with him.'

'You and your men did an excellent job,' the judge said. 'Tell your men to transfer the prisoner and the dead body to the guards I brought with me.' Rising, he added, 'I am really most grateful for your swift and efficient action, captain. This being a civilian case, you only needed to report the murder to the tribunal and you could have left it at that. You went out of your way to help me and . . .'

The captain raised his hand in a deprecatory gesture and said in his strange dull voice, 'It was a pleasure, sir. I happen to be one of Colonel Meng's men. We shall always do all we can to help you. All of us, always.'

The spasm that distorted his misshapen face had to be a smile. Judge Dee walked back to the guardhouse at the North Gate. He had decided to question the prisoner there at once, then go to the scene of the crime. If he transferred the investigation to the tribunal, clues might get stale. It seemed a fairly straightforward case, but one never knew.

He sat down at the only table in the bare guardroom and settled down to a study of the captain's report. It contained little beyond what the captain had already told him. The victim's full name was Choong Fang, age fifty-six; the girl was called Oriole, twenty years of age, and the young fisherman was twenty-two. He took the visiting-cards and the pawn-ticket from his sleeve. The cards stated that Mr Choong was a native of Shansi Province. The pawn-ticket was a tally, stamped with the large red stamp of Choong's pawnshop; it concerned four brocade robes pawned the day before by a Mrs Pei for three silver pieces, to be redeemed in three months at a monthly interest of 5 per cent.

The corporal came in, followed by two guards carrying the stretcher.

'Put it down there in the corner,' Judge Dee ordered. 'Do you know about that deaf-mute girl who lives in the watchtower? The military police gave only her personal name—Oriole.'

'Yes, sir, that's what she is called. She's an abandoned child. An old crone who used to sell fruit near the gate here brought her up and taught her to write a few dozen letters and a bit of sign language. When the old woman died two years ago, the girl went to live in the tower because the street urchins were always pestering her. She raises ducks there, and sells the eggs. People called her Oriole to make fun of her being dumb, and the nickname stuck.'

'All right. Bring the prisoner before me.'

The guards came back flanking a squat, sturdily built youngster. His tousled hair hung down over the corrugated brow of his swarthy, scowling face, and his brown jacket and trousers were clumsily patched in several places. His hands were chained behind his back, an extra loop of the thin chain encircling his thick, bare neck. The guards pressed him down on his knees in front of the judge.

Judge Dee observed the youngster in silence for a while, wondering what would be the best way to start the interrogation. There was only the patter of the rain outside, and the prisoner's heavy breathing. The judge took the three silver pieces from his sleeve.

'Where did you get these?'

The young fisherman muttered something in a broad dialect that the judge didn't quite understand. One of the guards kicked the prisoner and growled: 'Speak louder!'

'It's my savings. For buying a real boat.'

'When did you first meet Mr Choong?'

The boy burst out in a string of obscene curses. The guard on his right stopped him by hitting him over his head with the flat of his sword. Wang shook his head, then said dully, 'Only knew him by sight because he was often around on the quay.' Suddenly he added viciously: 'If I'd ever met him, I'd have killed the dirty swine, the crook . . .'

'Did Mr Choong cheat when you pawned something in his shop?' Judge Dee asked quickly.

'Think I have anything to pawn?'

'Why call him a crook then?'

Wang looked up at the judge who thought he caught a sly glint in his small, bloodshot eyes. The youngster bent his head again and replied in a sullen voice: 'Because all pawnbrokers are crooks.'

'What did you do last night?'

'I told the soldiers already. Had a bowl of noodles at the stall on the quay, then went up river. After I had caught some good fish, I moored the boat on the bank north of the tower and had a nap. I'd planned to bring some fish to the tower at dawn, for Oriole.'

Something in the way the boy pronounced the girl's name caught Judge Dee's attention. He said slowly, 'You deny having murdered the pawnbroker. Since, besides you, there was only the girl about, it follows it was she who killed him.'

Suddenly Wang jumped up and went for the judge. He moved so quickly that the two guards only got hold of him just in time. He kicked them but got a blow on his head that made him fall down backwards, his chains clanking on the floor-stones.

'You dog-official, you . . .' the youngster burst out, trying to scramble up. The corporal gave him a kick in the face that made his head slam back on the floor with a hard thud. He lay quite still, blood trickling from his torn mouth.

The judge got up and bent over the still figure. He had lost consciousness.

'Don't maltreat a prisoner unless you are ordered to,' the judge told the corporal sternly. 'Bring him round, and take him to the jail. Later I shall interrogate him formally, during the noon session. You'll take the dead body to the tribunal, corporal. Report to Sergeant Hoong and hand him this statement, drawn up by the captain of the military police. Tell the sergeant that I'll return to the tribunal as soon as I have questioned a few witnesses here.' He cast a look at the window. It was still raining. 'Get me a piece of oiled cloth!'

Before Judge Dee stepped outside he draped the oiled cloth over his head and shoulders, then jumped into the saddle of his hired horse. He rode along the quay and took the hardened road that led to the marshlands.

The mist had cleared a little and as he rode along he looked curiously at the deserted, green surface on either side of the road. Narrow gullies followed a winding course through the reeds, here and there broadening into large pools that gleamed dully in the grey light. A flight of small water birds suddenly flew up, with piercing cries that resounded eerily over the desolate marsh. He noticed that the water was subsiding after the torrential rain that had fallen in the night; the road was dry now, but the water had left large patches of duck-weed. When he was about to pass the blockhouse the sentry stopped him, but he let him go on as soon as the judge had shown him the identification document he carried in his boot.

The old watchtower was a clumsy, square building of five storeys, standing on a raised base of roughly hewn stone blocks. The shutters of the arched windows had gone and the roof of the top storey had caved in. Two big black crows sat perched on a broken beam.

As he came nearer he heard loud quacking. A few dozen ducks were huddling close together by the side of a muddy pool below the tower's base. When the judge dismounted and fastened the reins to a moss-covered stone pillar, the ducks began to splash around in the water, quacking indignantly.

The ground floor of the tower was just a dark, low vault, empty but for a heap of old broken furni̶̶̶̶̶̶̶̶ ̶̶ ̶̶ ̶̶arrow, rickety flight of wooden stairs led up to the floor ̶̶̶̶̶̶̶̶ ̶̶ ̶̶ ̶̶ he judge climbed up, seeking support with his left hand from the wet, mould-covered wall, for the bannisters were gone.

When he stepped into the half-dark, bare room, something stirred among the rags piled up on the roughly made plank-bed under the arched window. Some raucous sounds came from under a soiled, patched quilt. A quick look around showed that the room only contained a rustic table with a cracked teapot, and a bamboo bench against the side wall. In the corner was a brick oven carrying a large pan; beside it stood a rattan basket filled to the brim with pieces of charcoal. A musty smell of mould and stale sweat hung in the air.

Suddenly the quilt was thrown to the floor. A half-naked girl with long, tousled hair jumped down from the plank-bed. After one look at the judge, she again made that strange, raucous sound and scuttled to the farthest corner. Then she dropped to her knees, trembling violently.

Judge Dee realized that he didn't present a very reassuring sight. He quickly pulled his identification document from his boot, unfolded it and walked up to the cowering girl, pointing with his forefinger at the large red stamp of the tribunal. Then he pointed at himself.

She apparently understood, for now she scrambled up and stared at him with large eyes that held an animal fear. She wore nothing but a tattered skirt, fastened to her waist with a piece of straw rope. She had a shapely, well-developed body and her skin was surprisingly white. Her round face was smeared with dirt but was not unattractive. Judge Dee pulled the bench up to the table and sat down. Feeling that some familiar gesture was needed to reassure the frightened girl, he took the teapot and drank from the spout, as farmers do.

The girl came up to the table, spat on the dirty top and drew in the spittle with her forefinger a few badly deformed characters. They read: 'Wang did not kill him.'

The judge nodded. He poured tea on the table-top, and motioned her to wipe it clean. She obediently went to the bed, took a rag and began to polish the table top with feverish haste. Judge Dee

56

THEN SHE DROPPED TO HER KNEES, TREMBLING VIOLENTLY

walked over to the stove and selected a few pieces of charcoal. Resuming his seat, he wrote with the charcoal on the table-top: 'Who killed him?'

She shivered. She took the other piece of charcoal and wrote: 'Bad black goblins.' She pointed excitedly at the words, then scribbled quickly: 'Bad goblins changed the good rain spirit.'

'You saw the black goblins?' he wrote.

She shook her tousled head emphatically. She tapped with her forefinger repeatedly on the word 'black', then she pointed at her closed eyes and shook her head again. The judge sighed. He wrote: 'You know Mr Choong?'

She looked perplexedly at his writing, her finger in her mouth. He realized that the complicated character indicating the surname Choong was unknown to her. He crossed it out and wrote 'old man'.

She again shook her head. With an expression of disgust she drew circles round the words 'old man' and added: 'Too much blood. Good rain spirit won't come any more. No silver for Wang's boat any more.' Tears came trickling down her grubby cheeks as she wrote with a shaking hand: 'Good rain spirit always sleep with me.' She pointed at the plank-bed.

Judge Dee gave her a searching look. He knew that rain spirits played a prominent role in local folklore, so that it was only natural that they figured in the dreams and vagaries of this over-developed young girl. On the other hand, she had referred to silver. He wrote: 'What does the rain spirit look like?'

Her round face lit up. With a broad smile she wrote in big, clumsy letters: 'Tall. Handsome. Kind.' She drew a circle round each of the three words, then threw the charcoal on the table and, hugging her bare breasts, began to giggle ecstatically.

The judge averted his gaze. When he turned to look at her again, she had let her hands drop and stood there staring straight ahead with wide eyes. Suddenly her expression changed again. With a quick gesture she pointed at the arched window, and made some strange sounds. He turned round. There was a faint colour in the leaden sky, the trace of a rainbow. She stared at it, in childish delight, her mouth half open. The judge took up the

58

piece of charcoal for one final question: 'When does the rain spirit come?'

She stared at the words for a long time, absentmindedly combing her long, greasy locks with her fingers. At last she bent over the table and wrote: 'Black night and much rain.' She put circles round the words 'black' and 'rain', then added: 'He came with the rain.'

All at once she put her hands to her face and began to sob convulsively. The sound mingled with the loud quacking of the ducks from below. Realizing that she couldn't hear the birds, he rose and laid his hand on her bare shoulder. When she looked up he was shocked by the wild, half-crazed gleam in her wide eyes. He quickly drew a duck on the table, and added the word 'hunger'. She clasped her hand to her mouth and ran to the oven. Judge Dee scrutinized the large flagstones in front of the entrance. He saw there a clean space on the dirty, dust-covered floor. Evidently it was there that the dead man had lain, and the military police had swept up the floor. He remembered ruefully his unkind thoughts about them. Sounds of chopping made him turn round. The girl was cutting up stale rice cakes on a primitive chopping board. The judge watched with a worried frown her deft handling of the large kitchen knife. Suddenly she drove the long, sharp point of the knife in the board, then shook the chopped up rice cakes into the pan on the oven, giving the judge a happy smile over her shoulder. He nodded at her and went down the creaking stairs.

The rain had ceased, a thin mist was gathering over the marsh. While untying the reins, he told the noisy ducks: 'Don't worry, your breakfast is under way!'

He made his horse go ahead at a sedate pace. The mist came drifting in from the river. Strangely shaped clouds were floating over the tall reeds, here and there dissolving in long writhing trailers that resembled the tentacles of some monstrous water-animal. He wished he knew more about the hoary, deeply rooted beliefs of the local people. In many places people still venerated a river god or goddess, and farmers and fishermen made sacrificial offerings to these at the waterside. Evidently such things loomed large in the deaf-mute girl's feeble mind, shifting continually

59

from fact to fiction, and unable to control the urges of her full-blown body. He drove his horse to a gallop.

Back at the North Gate, he told the corporal to take him to the pawnbroker's place. When they had arrived at the large, prosperous-looking pawnshop the corporal explained that Choong's private residence was located directly behind the shop and pointed at the narrow alleyway that led to the main entrance. Judge Dee told the corporal he could go back, and knocked on the black-lacquered gate.

A lean man, neatly dressed in a brown gown with black sash and borders, opened it. Bestowing a bewildered look on his wet, bearded visitor, he said: 'You want the shop, I suppose. I can take you, I was just going there.'

'I am the magistrate,' Judge Dee told him impatiently. 'I've just come from the marsh. Had a look at the place where your partner was murdered. Let's go inside, I want to hand over to you what was found on the dead body.'

Mr Lin made a very low bow and conducted his distinguished visitor to a small but comfortable side hall, furnished in conventional style with a few pieces of heavy blackwood furniture. He ceremoniously led the judge to the broad bench at the back. While his host was telling the old manservant to bring tea and cakes, the judge looked curiously at the large aviary of copper wire on the wall table. About a dozen paddy birds were fluttering around inside.

'A hobby of my partner's,' Mr Lin said with an indulgent smile. 'He was very fond of birds, always fed them himself.'

With his neatly trimmed chin-beard and small, greying moustache Lin seemed at first sight just a typical middle-class shop-keeper. But a closer inspection revealed deep lines around his thin mouth, and large, sombre eyes that suggested a man with a definite personality. The judge set his cup down and formally expressed his sympathy with the firm's loss. Then he took the envelope from his sleeve and shook out the visiting-cards, the small cash, the pawn-ticket and the two keys. 'That's all, Mr Lin. Did your partner as a rule carry large sums of money on him?'

Lin silently looked the small pile over, stroking his chin-beard. 'No, sir. Since he retired from the firm two years ago, there was no need for him to carry much money about. But he certainly had more on him than just these few coppers when he went out last night.'

'What time was that?'

'About eight, sir. After we had had dinner together here downstairs. He wanted to take a walk along the quay, so he said.'

'Did Mr Choong often do that?'

'Oh yes, sir! He had always been a man of solitary habits, and after the demise of his wife two years ago, he went out for long walks nearly every other night and always by himself. He always had his meals served in his small library upstairs, although I live here in this same house, in the left wing. Last night, however, there was a matter of business to discuss and therefore he came down to have dinner with me.'

'You have no family, Mr Lin?'

'No, sir. Never had time to establish a household! My partner had the capital, but the actual business of the pawnshop he left largely to me. And after his retirement he hardly set foot in our shop.'

'I see. To come back to last night. Did Mr Choong say when he would be back?'

'No, sir. The servant had standing orders not to wait up for him. My partner was an enthusiastic fisherman, you see. If he thought it looked like good fishing weather on the quay, he would hire a boat and pass the night up river.'

Judge Dee nodded slowly. 'The military police will have told you that they arrested a young fisherman called Wang San-lang. Did your partner often hire his boat?'

'That I don't know, sir. There are scores of fishermen about on the quay, you see, and most of them are eager to make a few extra coppers. But if my partner rented Wang's boat, it doesn't astonish me that he ran into trouble, for Wang is a violent young ruffian. I know of him, because being a fisherman of sorts myself, I have often heard the others talk about him. Surly, uncompanionable youngster.' He sighed. 'I'd like to go out fishing as often as my partner did, only I haven't got that much time. . . . Well, it's very kind of you to have brought these keys, sir. Lucky that Wang didn't take them and throw them away! The larger one is the key of my late partner's library, the other of the strongbox he has there for keeping important papers.' He stretched out his hand to take the keys, but Judge Dee scooped them up and put them in his sleeve.

'Since I am here,' he said, 'I shall have a look at Mr Choong's papers right now, Mr Lin. This is a murder case, and until it is solved, all the victim's papers are temporarily at the disposal of the authorities for possible clues. Take me to the library, please.'

'Certainly, sir.' Lin took the judge up a broad staircase and pointed at the door at the end of the corridor. The judge unlocked it with the larger key.

'Thanks very much, Mr Lin. I shall join you downstairs presently.'

The judge stepped into the small room, locked the door behind him, then went to push the low, broad window wide open. The roofs of the neighbouring houses gleamed in the grey mist. He turned and sat down in the capacious armchair behind the rosewood writing-desk facing the window. After a casual look at the iron-bound strongbox on the floor beside his chair, he leaned back and pensively took stock of his surroundings. The small library was scrupulously clean and furnished with simple, old-fashioned taste. The spotless whitewashed walls were decorated with two good landscape scrolls, and the solid ebony wall table bore a slender vase of white porcelain, with a few wilting roses. Piles of books in brocade covers were neatly stacked on the shelves of the small bookcase of spotted bamboo.

Folding his arms, the judge wondered what connection there could be between this tastefully arranged library that seemed to belong to an elegant scholar rather than to a pawnbroker, and the bare, dark room in the half-ruined watchtower, breathing decay, sloth and the direst poverty. After a while he shook his head, bent and unlocked the strongbox. Its contents matched the methodical neatness of the room: bundles of documents, each bound up with green ribbon and provided with an inscribed label. He selected the bundles marked 'private correspondence' and 'accounts and receipts'. The former contained a few important letters about capital investment and correspondence from his sons, mainly about their family affairs and asking Mr Choong's advice and instructions. Leafing through the second bundle, Judge Dee's practised eye saw at once that the deceased had been leading a frugal, nearly austere life. Suddenly he frowned. He had found a pink receipt, bearing the stamp of a house of assignation. It was dated back a year and a half. He quickly went through the bundle and found half a dozen similar receipts, the last dated back six months. Apparently Mr Choong had, after his wife's demise, hoped to find consolation in venal love, but had soon discovered that such hope was vain. With a sigh he opened the large envelope which he had taken from the bottom of the box. It was marked: 'Last Will and Testament'. It was dated one year before, and stated that all of Mr Choong's landed property—which was considerable—was to go to his two sons, together with two-thirds of his capital. The remaining one-third, and the pawnshop, was bequeathed to Mr Lin 'in recognition of his long and loyal service to the firm'.

The judge replaced the papers. He rose and went to inspect the bookcase. He discovered that except for two dog-eared dictionaries, all the books were collections of poetry, complete editions of the most representative lyrical poets of former times. He looked through one volume. Every difficult word had been annotated in red ink, in an unformed, rather clumsy hand. Nodding slowly, he replaced the volume. Yes, now he understood. Mr Choong had been engaged in a trade that forbade all personal feeling, namely that of a pawnbroker. And his pronouncedly ugly face made tender attachments unlikely. Yet at heart he was a romantic, hankering after the higher things of life, but very self-conscious and shy about these yearnings. As a merchant he had of course only received an elementary education, so he tried laboriously to expand his literary knowledge, reading old poetry with a dictionary in this small library which he kept so carefully locked.

Judge Dee sat down again and took his folding fan from his sleeve. Fanning himself, he concentrated his thoughts on this unusual pawnbroker. The only glimpse the outer world got of the sensitive nature of this man was his love of birds, evinced by the paddy birds downstairs. At last the judge got up. About to put his fan back into his sleeve, he suddenly checked himself. He looked at the fan absentmindedly for a while, then laid it on the desk. After a last look at the room he went downstairs.

His host offered him another cup of tea but Judge Dee shook his head. Handing Lin the two keys, he said, 'I have to go back to the tribunal now. I found nothing among your partner's papers suggesting that he had any enemies, so I think that this case is exactly what it seems, namely a case of murder for gain. To a poor man, three silver pieces are a fortune. Why are those birds fluttering about?' He went to the cage. 'Aha, their water is dirty. You ought to tell the servant to change it, Mr Lin.'

Lin muttered something and clapped his hands. Judge Dee groped in his sleeve. 'How careless of me!' he exclaimed. 'I left my fan on the desk upstairs. Would you fetch it for me, Mr Lin?'

Just as Lin was rushing to the staircase, the old manservant came in. When the judge had told him that the water in the reservoir of the birdcage ought to be changed daily, the old man said, shaking his head, 'I told Mr Lin so, but he wouldn't listen. Doesn't care for birds. My master now, he loved them, he . . .'

'Yes, Mr Lin told me that last night he had an argument with your master about those birds.'

'Well yes, sir, both of them got quite excited. What was it about, sir? I only caught a few words about birds when I brought the rice.'

'It doesn't matter,' the judge said quickly. He had heard Mr Lin come downstairs. 'Well, Mr Lin, thanks for the tea. Come to the chancery in, say, one hour, with the most important documents relating to your late partner's assets. My senior clerk will help you fill out the official forms, and the registration of Mr Choong's will.'

Mr Lin thanked the judge profusely and saw him respectfully to the door.

Judge Dee told the guards at the gate of the tribunal to return his rented horse to the blacksmith, and went straight to his private residence at the back of the chancery. The old housemaster informed him that Sergeant Hoong was waiting in his private office. The judge nodded. 'Tell the bathroom attendant that I want to take a bath now.'

In the black-tiled dressing-room adjoining the bath he quickly stripped off his robe, drenched with sweat and rain. He felt soiled, in body and in mind. The attendant sluiced him with cold water, and vigorously scrubbed his back. But it was only after the judge had been lying in the sunken pool in hot water for some time that he began to feel better. Thereafter he had the attendant massage his shoulders, and when he had been rubbed dry he put on a crisp clean robe of blue cotton, and placed a cap of thin black gauze on his head. In this attire he walked over to his women's quarters.

About to enter the garden room where his ladies usually passed the morning, he halted a moment, touched by the peaceful scene. His two wives, clad in flowered robes of thin silk, were sitting with Miss Tsao at the red-lacquered table in front of the open sliding doors. The walled-in rock garden outside, planted with ferns and tall, rustling bamboos, suggested refreshing coolness. This was his own private world, a clean haven of refuge from the outside world of cruel violence and repulsive decadence he had to deal with in his official life. Then and there he took the firm resolution that he would preserve his harmonious family life intact, always.

His First Lady put her embroidery frame down and quickly came to meet him. 'We have been waiting with breakfast for you for nearly an hour!' she told him reproachfully.

'I am sorry. The fact is that there was some trouble at the North Gate and I had to attend to it at once. I must go to the chancery now, but I shall join you for the noon rice.' She conducted him to the door. When she was making her bow he told her in a low voice, 'By the way, I have decided to follow your advice in the matter we discussed last night. Please make the necessary arrangements.'

With a pleased smile she bowed again, and the judge went down the corridor that led to the chancery.

He found Sergeant Hoong sitting in an armchair in the corner of his private office. His old adviser got up and wished him a good morning. Tapping the document in his hand, the sergeant said, 'I was relieved when I got this report, Your Honour, for we were getting worried about your prolonged absence! I had the prisoner locked up in jail, and the dead body deposited in the mortuary. After I had viewed it with the coroner, Ma Joong and

Chiao Tai, your two lieutenants, rode to the North Gate to see whether you needed any assistance.'

Judge Dee had sat down behind his desk. He looked askance at the pile of dossiers. 'Is there anything urgent among the incoming documents, Hoong?'

'No, sir. All those files concern routine administrative matters.'

'Good. Then we shall devote the noon session to the murder of the pawnbroker Choong.'

The sergeant nodded contentedly. 'I saw from the captain's report, Your Honour, that it is a fairly simple case. And since we have the murder suspect safely under lock and key . . .'

The judge shook his head. 'No, Hoong, I wouldn't call it a simple case, exactly. But thanks to the quick measures of the military police, and thanks to the lucky chance that brought me right into the middle of things, a definite pattern has emerged.'

He clapped his hands. When the headman came inside and made his bow the judge ordered him to bring the prisoner Wang before him. He went on to the sergeant, 'I am perfectly aware, Hoong, that a judge is supposed to interrogate an accused only publicly, in court. But this is not a formal hearing. A general talk for my orientation, rather.'

Sergeant Hoong looked doubtful, but the judge vouchsafed no further explanation, and began to leaf through the topmost file on his desk. He looked up when the headman brought Wang inside. The chains had been taken off him, but his swarthy face looked as surly as before. The headman pressed him down on his knees, then stood himself behind him, his heavy whip in his hands.

'Your presence is not required, Headman,' Judge Dee told him curtly.

The headman cast a worried glance at Sergeant Hoong. 'This is a violent ruffian, Your Honour,' he began diffidently. 'He might . . .'

'You heard me!' the judge snapped.

After the disconcerted headman had left, Judge Dee leaned back in his chair. He asked the young fisherman in a conversational tone, 'How long have you been living on the waterfront, Wang?'

'Ever since I can remember,' the boy muttered.

'It's a strange land,' the judge said slowly to Sergeant Hoong. 'When I was riding through the marsh this morning, I saw weirdly shaped clouds drifting about, and shreds of mist that looked like long arms reaching up out of the water, as if . . .'

The youngster had been listening intently. Now he interrupted quickly : 'Better not speak of those things !'

'Yes, you know all about those things, Wang. On stormy nights, there must be more going on in the marshlands than we city-dwellers realize.'

Wang nodded vigorously. 'I've seen many things,' he said in a low voice, 'with my own eyes. They all come up from the water. Some can harm you, others help drowning people, sometimes. But it's better to keep away from them, anyway.'

'Exactly ! Yet you made bold to interfere, Wang. And see what has happened to you now ! You were arrested, you were kicked and beaten, and now you are a prisoner accused of murder !'

'I told you I didn't kill him !'

'Yes. But did you know who or what killed him ? Yet you stabbed him when he was dead. Several times.'

'I saw red . . .' Wang muttered. 'If I'd known sooner, I'd have cut his throat. For I know him by sight, the rat, the . . .'

'Hold your tongue !' Judge Dee interrupted him sharply. 'You cut up a dead man, and that's a mean and cowardly thing to do !' He continued, calmer, 'However, since even in your blind rage you spared Oriole by refraining from an explanation, I am willing to forget what you did. How long have you been going with her ?'

'Over a year. She's sweet, and she's clever too. Don't believe she's a half-wit ! She can write more than a hundred characters. I can read only a dozen or so.'

Judge Dee took the three silver pieces from his sleeve and laid them on the desk. 'Take this silver, it belongs rightly to her and to you. Buy your boat and marry her. She needs you, Wang.' The youngster snatched the silver and tucked it in his belt. The judge went on, 'You'll have to go back to jail for a few hours, for I can't release you until you have been formally cleared of the murder charge. Then you'll be set free. Learn to control your temper, Wang!'

He clapped his hands. The headman came in at once. He had been waiting just outside the door, ready to rush inside at the first sign of trouble.

'Take the prisoner back to his cell, headman. Then fetch Mr Lin. You'll find him in the chancery.'

Sergeant Hoong had been listening with mounting astonishment. Now he asked with a perplexed look, 'What were you talking about with that young fellow, Your Honour? I couldn't follow it at all. Are you really intending to let him go?'

Judge Dee rose and went to the window. Looking out at the dreary, wet courtyard, he said, 'It's raining again! What was I talking about, Hoong? I was just checking whether Wang really believed all those weird superstitions. One of these days, Hoong, you might try to find in our chancery library a book on local folklore.'

'But you don't believe all that nonsense, sir!'

'No, I don't. Not all of it, at least. But I feel I ought to read up on the subject, for it plays a large role in the daily life of the common people of our district. Pour me a cup of tea, will you?'

While the sergeant prepared the tea, Judge Dee resumed his seat and concentrated on the official documents on his desk. After he had drunk a second cup, there was a knock at the door. The headman ushered Mr Lin inside, then discreetly withdrew.

'Sit down, Mr Lin!' the judge addressed his guest affably. 'I trust my senior clerk gave you the necessary instructions for the documents to be drawn up?'

'Yes, indeed, Your Honour. Right now we were checking the landed property with the register and . . .'

'According to the will drawn up a year ago,' the judge cut in, 'Mr Choong bequeathed all the land to his two sons, together with two-thirds of his capital, as you know. One-third of the capital, and the pawnshop, he left to you. Are you planning to continue the business?'

'No, sir,' Lin replied with his thin smile. 'I have worked in that pawnshop for more than thirty years, from morning till night. I shall sell it, and live off the rent from my capital.'

'Precisely. But suppose Mr Choong had made a new will? Containing a new clause stipulating that you were to get only the shop?' As Lin's face went livid, he went on quickly, 'It's a prosperous business, but it would take you four or five years to assemble enough capital to retire. And you are getting on in years, Mr Lin.'

'Impossible! How . . . how could he . . .' Lin stammered. Then he snapped, 'Did you find a new will in his strongbox?'

Instead of answering the question, Judge Dee said coldly: 'Your partner had a mistress, Mr Lin. Her love came to mean more to him than anything else.'

Lin jumped up. 'Do you mean to say that the old fool willed his money to that deaf-mute slut?'

'Yes, you know all about that affair, Mr Lin. Since last night, when your partner told you. You had a violent quarrel. No, don't try to deny it! Your manservant overheard what you said, and he will testify in court.'

Lin sat down again. He wiped his moist face. Then he began, calmer now, 'Yes, sir, I admit that I got very angry when my partner informed me last night that he loved that girl. He wanted to take her away to some distant place and marry her. I tried to make him see how utterly foolish that would be, but he told me to mind my own business and ran out of the house in a huff. I had no idea he would go to the tower. It's common knowledge that that young hoodlum Wang is carrying on with the half-wit. Wang surprised the two, and he murdered my partner. I apologize for not having mentioned these facts to you this morning, sir. I couldn't bring myself to compromise my late partner. . . . And since you had arrested the murderer, everything would have come out anyway in court. . . .' He shook his head. 'I am partly to blame, sir. I should have gone after him last night, I should've . . .'

'But you did go after him, Mr Lin,' Judge Dee interrupted curtly. 'You are a fisherman too, you know the marsh as well as your partner. Ordinarily one can't cross the marsh, but after a heavy rain the water rises, and an experienced boatman in a shallow skiff could paddle across by way of the swollen gullies and pools.'

'Impossible! The road is patrolled by the military police all night!'

'A man crouching in a skiff could take cover behind the tall reeds, Mr Lin. Therefore your partner could only visit the tower on nights after a heavy rain. And therefore the poor half-witted girl took the visitor for a supernatural being, a rain spirit. For he came with the rain.' He sighed. Suddenly he fixed Lin with his piercing eyes and said sternly, 'When Mr Choong told you about his plans last night, Lin, you saw all your long-cherished hopes of a life in ease and luxury go up into thin air. Therefore you followed Choong, and you murdered him in the tower by thrusting a knife into his back.'

Lin raised his hands. 'What a fantastic theory, sir! How do you propose to prove this slanderous accusation?'

'By Mrs Pei's pawn-ticket, among other things. It was found by the military police on the scene of the crime. But Mr Choong had completely retired from the business, as you told me yourself. Why then would he be carrying a pawn-ticket that had been issued that very day?' As Lin remained silent, Judge Dee went on, 'You decided on the spur of the moment to murder Choong, and you rushed after him. It was the hour after the evening rice, so the shopkeepers in your neighbourhood were on the lookout for their evening custom when you passed. Also on the quay, where you took off in your small skiff, there were an unusual number of people about, because it looked like heavy rain was on its way.' The glint of sudden panic in Lin's eyes was the last confirmation the judge had been waiting for. He concluded in an even voice, 'If you confess now, Mr Lin, sparing me the trouble of sifting out all the evidence of the eyewitnesses, I am prepared to add a plea for clemency to your death sentence, on the ground that it was unpremeditated murder.'

Lin stared ahead with a vacant look. All at once his pale face became distorted by a spasm of rage. 'The despicable old lecher!' he spat. 'Made me sweat and slave all those years . . . and now he was going to throw all that good money away on a cheap, half-witted slut! The money I made for him. . . .' He looked steadily at the judge as he added in a firm voice, 'Yes, I killed him. He deserved it.'

Judge Dee gave the sergeant a sign. While Hoong went to the door the judge told the pawnbroker, 'I shall hear your full confession during the noon session.'

They waited in silence till the sergeant came back with the headman and two constables. They put Lin in chains and led him away.

'A sordid case, sir,' Sergeant Hoong remarked dejectedly.

The judge took a sip from his teacup and held it up to be refilled. 'Pathetic, rather. I would even call Lin pathetic, Hoong, were it not for the fact that he made a determined effort to incriminate Wang.'

'What was Wang's role in all this, sir? You didn't even ask him what he did this morning!'

'There was no need to, for what happened is as plain as a pikestaff. Oriole had told Wang that a rain spirit visited her at night and sometimes gave her money. Wang considered it a great honour that she had relations with a rain spirit. Remember that only half a century ago in many of the river districts in our Empire the people immolated every year a young boy or girl as a human sacrifice to the local river god—until the authorities stepped in. When Wang came to the tower this morning to bring Oriole her fish, he found in her room a dead man lying on his face on the floor. The crying Oriole gave him to understand that goblins had killed the rain spirit and changed him into an ugly old man. When Wang turned over the corpse and recognized the old man, he suddenly understood that he and Oriole had been deceived, and in a blind rage pulled his knife and stabbed the dead man. Then he realized that this was a murder case and he would be suspected. So he fled. The military police caught him while trying to wash his trousers which had become stained with Choong's blood.'

Sergeant Hoong nodded. 'How did you discover all this in only a few hours, sir?'

'At first I thought the captain's theory hit the nail on the head. The only point which worried me a bit was the long interval between the murder and the stabbing of the victim's breast. I didn't worry a bit about the pawn-ticket, for it is perfectly normal for a pawnbroker to carry a ticket about that he has made

71

out that very same day. Then, when questioning Wang, it struck me that he called Choong a crook. That was a slip of the tongue, for Wang was determined to keep both Oriole and himself out of this, so as not to have to divulge that they had let themselves be fooled. While I was interviewing Oriole she stated that the "goblins" had killed and *changed* her rain spirit. I didn't understand that at all. It was during my visit to Lin that at last I got on the right track. Lin was nervous and therefore garrulous, and told me at length about his partner taking no part at all in the business. I remembered the pawn-ticket found on the murder scene, and began to suspect Lin. But it was only after I had inspected the dead man's library and got a clear impression of his personality that I found the solution. I checked my theory by eliciting from the manservant the fact that Lin and Choong had quarreled about Oriole the night before. The name Oriole meant of course nothing to the servant, but he told me they had a heated argument about birds. The rest was routine.'

The judge put his cup down. 'I have learned from this case how important it is to study carefully our ancient handbooks of detection, Hoong. There it is stated again and again that the first step of a murder investigation is to ascertain the character, daily life and habits of the victim. And in this case it was indeed the murdered man's personality that supplied the key.'

Sergeant Hoong stroked his grey moustache with a pleased smile. 'That girl and her young man were very lucky indeed in having you as the investigating magistrate, sir ! For all the evidence pointed straight at Wang, and he would have been convicted and beheaded. For the girl is a deaf-mute, and Wang isn't much of a talker either !'

Judge Dee nodded. Leaning back in his chair, he said with a faint smile :

'That brings me to the main benefit I derived from this case, Hoong. A very personal and very important benefit. I must confess to you that early this morning I was feeling a bit low, and for a moment actually doubted whether this was after all the right career for me. I was a fool. This is a great, a magnificent office, Hoong ! If only because it enables us to speak for those who can't speak for themselves.'

THE MURDER ON THE LOTUS POND

This case occurred in the year A.D. 667 in Han-yuan, an
ancient little town built on the shore of a lake near the
capital. There Judge Dee has to solve the murder of an elderly
poet, who lived in retirement on his modest property behind
the Willow Quarter, the abode of the courtesans and singing-
girls. The poet was murdered while peacefully contemplating
the moon in his garden pavilion, set in the centre of a lotus
pond. There were no witnesses—or so it seemed.

From the small pavilion in the centre of the lotus pond he coul
survey the entire garden, bathed in moonlight. He listened ir
tently. Everything remained quiet. With a satisfied smile h
looked down at the dead man in the bamboo chair, at the hilt c
the knife sticking up from his breast. Only a few drops of bloo
trickled down the grey cloth of his robe. The man took up on
of the two porcelain cups that stood by the pewter wine jar or
the round table. He emptied it at one draught, then muttered t
the corpse, 'Rest in peace ! If you had been only a fool, I woul
probably have spared you. But since you were an interferin
fool . . .'

He shrugged his shoulders. All had gone well. It was past mic
night; no one would come to this lonely country house on th
outskirts of the city. And in the dark house at the other end c
the garden nothing stirred. He examined his hands—there wa
no trace of blood. Then he stooped and scrutinized the floor c
the pavilion, and the chair he had been sitting on opposite th
dead man. No, he hadn't left any clue. He could leave now, a
was safe.

Suddenly, he heard a plopping sound behind him. He swun
round, startled. Then he sighed with relief; it was only a larg
green frog. It had jumped up out of the pond on to the marb'
steps of the pavilion. Now it sat there looking up at him solemn'
with its blinking, protruding eyes.

'You can't talk, bastard !' the man sneered. 'But I'll ma

louble-sure!' So speaking, he gave the frog a vicious kick that smashed it against the table leg. The animal's long hindlegs twitched, then it lay still. The man picked up the second wine cup, the one his victim had been drinking from. He examined it, then he put it in his wide sleeve. Now he was ready. As he turned to go, his eye fell on the dead frog.

'Join your comrades!' he said with contempt and kicked it into the water. It fell with a splash among the lotus plants. At once the croaking of hundreds of frightened frogs tore the quiet night.

The man cursed violently. He quickly crossed the curved bridge that led over the pond to the garden gate. After he had slipped outside and pulled the gate shut, the frogs grew quiet again.

A few hours later three horsemen were riding along the lake road, back to the city. The red glow of dawn shone on their brown hunting-robes and black caps. A cool morning breeze rippled the surface of the lake, but soon it would grow hot, for it was mid-summer.

The broad-shouldered, bearded man said with a smile to his thin, elderly companion, 'Our duck-hunt suggested a good method for catching wily criminals! You set up a decoy, then stay in hiding with your clap-net ready. When your bird shows up, you net him!'

Four peasants walking in the opposite direction quickly set down the loads of vegetables they were carrying, and knelt down by the roadside. They had recognized the bearded man: it was Judge Dee, the magistrate of the lake-district of Han-yuan.

'We did a powerful lot of clapping among the reeds, sir,' the stalwart man who was riding behind them remarked wryly. 'But all we got was a few waterplants!'

'Anyway it was good exercise, Ma Joong!' Judge Dee said over his shoulder to his lieutenant. Then he went on to the thin man riding by his side: 'If we did this every morning, Mr Yuan, we'd never need your pills and powders!'

The thin man smiled bleakly. His name was Yuan Kai, and he was the wealthy owner of the largest pharmacy in Judge Dee's district. Duck-hunting was his favourite sport.

Judge Dee drove his horse on, and soon they entered the city of Han-yuan, built against the mountain slope. At the market place, in front of the Temple of Confucius, the three men dismounted; then they climbed the stone steps leading up to the street where the tribunal stood, overlooking the city and the lake.

Ma Joong pointed at the squat man standing in front of the monumental gate of the tribunal. 'Heavens!' he growled, 'I have never seen our good headman up so early. I fear he must be gravely ill!'

The headman of the constables came running towards them. He made a bow, then said excitedly to the judge, 'The poet Meng Lan has been murdered, Your Honour! Half an hour ago his servant came rushing here and reported that he had found his master's dead body in the garden pavilion.'

'Meng Lan? A poet?' Judge Dee said with a frown. 'In the year I have been here in Han-yuan I have never even heard the name.'

'He lives in an old country house, near the marsh to the east of the city, sir,' the pharmacist said. 'He is not very well known here; he rarely comes to the city. But I heard that in the capital his poetry is praised highly by connoisseurs.'

'We'd better go there at once,' the judge said. 'Have Sergeant Hoong and my two other lieutenants come back yet, Headman?'

'No sir, they are still in the village near the west boundary of our district. Just after Your Honour left this morning, a man came with a note from Sergeant Hoong. It said that they hadn't yet found a single clue to the men who robbed the treasury messenger.'

Judge Dee tugged at his long beard. 'That robbery is a vexing case!' he said testily. 'The messenger was carrying a dozen gold bars. And now we have a murder on our hands too! Well, we'll manage, Ma Joong. Do you know the way to the dead poet's country place?'

'I know a short-cut through the east quarter, sir,' Yuan Kai said. 'If you'll allow me . . .'

'By all means! You come along too, Headman. You sent a couple of constables back with Meng's servant to see that nothing is disturbed, I trust?'

75

'I certainly did, sir!' the headman said importantly.

'You are making progress,' Judge Dee observed. Seeing the headman's smug smile, he added dryly, 'A pity that the progress is so slow. Get four horses from the stables!'

The pharmacist rode ahead and led them along several narrow alleys, zigzagging down to the bank of the lake. Soon they were riding through a lane lined with willow trees. These had given their name to the Willow Quarter, the abode of the dancing-girls and courtesans that lay to the east of the city.

'Tell me about Meng Lan,' the judge said to the pharmacist.

'I didn't know him too well, sir. I visited him only three or four times, but he seemed a nice, modest kind of person. He settled down here two years ago, in an old country house behind the Willow Quarter. It has only three rooms or so, but there is a beautiful large garden, with a lotus pond.'

'Has he got a large family?'

'No sir, he was a widower when he came here; his two grown-up sons live in the capital. Last year he met a courtesan from the Willow Quarter. He bought her out, and married her. She didn't have much to commend herself besides her looks—she can't read or write, sing or dance. Meng Lan was able to buy her cheaply, therefore, but it took all his savings. He was living on a small annuity an admirer in the capital was sending him. I am told it was a happy marriage, although Meng was of course much older than she.'

'One would have thought,' Judge Dee remarked, 'that a poet would choose an educated girl who could share his literary interests.'

'She is a quiet, soft-spoken woman, sir,' the pharmacist said with a shrug. 'And she looked after him well.'

'Meng Lan was a smart customer, even though he wrote poetry,' Ma Joong muttered. 'A nice, quiet girl that looks after you well—a man can hardly do better than that!'

The willow lane had narrowed to a pathway. It led through the high oak trees and thick undergrowth that marked the vicinity of the marsh behind the Willow Quarter.

The four men dismounted in front of a rustic bamboo gate. The two constables standing guard there saluted, then pushed the gate open. Before entering, Judge Dee surveyed the large garden. It was not very well kept. The flowering shrubs and bushes round the lotus pond were running wild, but they gave the place a kind of savage beauty. Some butterflies were fluttering lazily over the large lotus leaves that covered the pond's surface.

'Meng Lan was very fond of this garden,' Yuan Kai remarked.

The judge nodded. He looked at the red-lacquered wooden bridge that led over the water to a hexagonal pavilion, open on all sides. Slender pillars supported the pointed roof, decked with green tiles. Beyond the pond, at the back of the garden, he saw a low, rambling wooden building. Its thatched roof was half covered by the low foliage of the tall oak trees that stood behind the house.

It was getting very hot. Judge Dee wiped the perspiration from his brow and crossed the narrow bridge, the three others following behind him. The small pavilion offered hardly enough space for the four men. Judge Dee stood looking for a while at the thin figure, clad in a simple house-robe of grey cloth, lying back in the bamboo armchair. Then he felt the shoulders, and the limp arms. Righting himself, he said, 'The body is just getting stiff. In this hot, humid weather it's hard to fix the time of death. In any case after midnight, I would say.' He carefully pulled the knife out of the dead man's breast. He examined the long, thin blade and the plain ivory hilt. Ma Joong pursed his lips and said, 'Won't help us much, sir. Every ironmonger in town keeps these cheap knives in stock.'

Judge Dee silently handed the knife to him. Ma Joong wrapped it up in a sheet of paper he had taken from his sleeve. The judge studied the thin face of the dead man. It was frozen in an eery, lopsided grin. The poet had a long, ragged moustache and a wispy grey goatee; the judge put his age at about sixty. He took the large wine jar from the table and shook it. Only a little wine was left. Then he picked up the wine cup standing next to it, and examined it. With a puzzled look he put it in his sleeve. Turning to the headman he said:

'Tell the constables to make a stretcher of some branches, and convey the body to the tribunal, for the autopsy.' And to Yuan Kai: 'You might sit on that stone bench over there near the

77

fence for a while, Mr Yuan. I won't be long.' He motioned Ma Joong to follow him.

They crossed the bridge again. The thin planks creaked under the weight of the two heavy men. They walked round the lotus pond and on to the house. With relief Judge Dee inhaled the cool air in the shadow under the porch. Ma Joong knocked.

A rather handsome but surly-looking youngster opened. Ma Joong told him that the magistrate wanted to see Mrs Meng. As the boy went hurriedly inside, Judge Dee sat down at the rickety bamboo table in the centre of the sparsely furnished room. Ma Joong stood with folded arms behind his chair. The judge took in the old, worn furniture, and the cracked plaster walls. He said, 'Robbery can't have been the motive, evidently.'

'There—the motive is coming, sir!' Ma Joong whispered. 'Old husband, pretty young wife—we know the rest!'

Judge Dee looked round and saw that a slender woman of about twenty-five had appeared in the door opening. Her face was not made up and her cheeks showed the traces of tears. But her large, liquid eyes, gracefully curved eyebrows, full red lips and smooth complexion made her a very attractive woman. The robe she wore was of faded blue cloth, but it did not conceal her splendid figure. After one frightened look at the judge she made an obeisance, then remained standing there with downcast eyes, waiting respectfully till he would address her.

'I am distressed, madam,' Judge Dee said in a gentle voice, 'that I have to bother you so soon after the tragedy. I trust that you'll understand, however, that I must take swift action to bring the vile murderer to justice.' As she nodded he went on: 'When did you see your husband last?'

'We had our evening rice here in this room,' Mrs Meng replied in a soft, melodious voice. 'Thereafter, when I had cleared the table, my husband read here for a few hours, and then said that since there was a beautiful moon he would go to the garden pavilion and have a few cups of wine there.'

'Did he often do that?'

'Oh yes, he would go out there nearly every other night, enjoying the cool evening breeze, and humming songs.'

'Did he often receive visitors there?'

'Never, Your Honour. He liked to be left alone, and did not encourage visitors. The few people who came to see him he always received in the afternoon, and here in the hall, for a cup of tea. I loved this peaceful life, my husband was so considerate, he . . .'

Her eyes became moist and her mouth twitched. But soon she took hold of herself and went on, 'I prepared a large jar of warm wine, and brought it out to the pavilion. My husband said that I need not wait up for him, since he planned to be sitting there till a late hour. Thus I went to bed. Early this morning the servant knocked frantically on the door of our bedroom. I then saw that my husband wasn't there. The boy told me that he had found him in the pavilion. . . .'

'Does this boy live here in the house?' Judge Dee asked.

'No, Your Honour, he stays with his father, the gardener of the largest house in the Willow Quarter. The boy only comes for the day; he leaves after I have prepared the evening rice.'

'Did you hear anything unusual during the night?'

Mrs Meng frowned, then answered, 'I woke up once, it must have been shortly after midnight. The frogs in the pond were making a terrible noise. During the daytime one never hears them, they stay under water. Even when I wade into the pond to gather lotus flowers they remain quiet. But at night they come out, and they are easily startled. Therefore I thought that my husband was coming inside, and had dropped a stone or so into the pond. Then I dozed off again.'

'I see,' Judge Dee said. He thought for a while, caressing his long sidewhiskers. 'Your husband's face didn't show any signs of terror or astonishment; he must have been stabbed quite unexpectedly. He was dead before he knew what was happening. That proves your husband knew his murderer well; they must have been sitting there drinking wine together. The large jar was nearly empty, but there was only one cup. I suppose that it would be difficult to check whether a wine cup is missing?'

'It's not difficult at all,' Mrs Meng replied with a thin smile. 'We have only seven cups, a set of six, of green porcelain, and one larger cup of white porcelain, which my husband always used.'

The judge raised his eyebrows. The cup he had found was of green porcelain. He resumed: 'Did your husband have any enemies?'

'None, Your Honour!' she exclaimed. 'I can't understand who . . .'

'Do *you* have enemies?' Judge Dee interrupted.

She grew red in the face, and bit her lip. Then she said contritely, 'Of course Your Honour knows that until a year ago I worked in the quarter over there. Occasionally I refused a person who sought my favours, but I am certain that none of them would ever . . . And after all that time . . .' Her voice trailed off.

The judge rose. He thanked Mrs Meng, expressed his sympathy, and took his leave.

When the two men were walking down the garden path Ma Joong said, 'You ought to have asked her also about her *friends*, sir!'

'I depend on you for that information, Ma Joong. Have you kept in contact with that girl from the quarter—Apple Blossom is her name, I think.'

'Peach Blossom, sir. Certainly I have!'

'Good. You'll go to the quarter right now, and get her to tell you everything she knows about Mrs Meng at the time she was still working there. Especially about the men she used to associate with.'

'It's very early in the day, sir,' Ma Joong said doubtfully. 'She'll still be asleep.'

'Then you wake her up! Get going!'

Ma Joong looked dejected, but he hurried to the gate. Judge Dee reflected idly that if he sent his amorous lieutenant often enough to interview his lady-friends before breakfast, he might yet cure him of his weakness. As a rule such women don't look their best in the early morning after a late night.

Yuan Kai was standing by the lotus pond talking earnestly with a newcomer, a tall, neatly dressed man with a heavy-jowled, rather solemn face. The pharmacist introduced him as Mr Wen Shou-fang, newly elected master of the tea-merchants' guild. The guildmaster made a low bow, then began an elaborate apology for not having called on the judge yet. Judge Dee cut him short, asking, 'What brings you here so early in the morning, Mr Wen?'

Wen seemed taken aback by this sudden question. He stammered, 'I . . . I wanted to express my sympathy to Mrs Meng, and . . . to ask her whether I could help her in any way. . . .'

'So you knew the Mengs well?' Judge Dee asked.

'I was just talking this matter over with my friend Wen, sir,' Yuan Kai interposed hurriedly. 'We decided to report to Your Honour here and now that both Wen and I myself sought Mrs Meng's favours when she was still a courtesan, and that neither of us was successful. Both of us want to state that we perfectly understood that a courtesan is free to grant or withhold her favours, and that neither of us bore her any malice. Also that we had a high regard for Meng Lan, and were very glad that their marriage proved to turn out so well. Therefore . . .'

'Just to get the record straight,' the judge interrupted, 'I suppose that both of you can prove that you weren't in this vicinity last night?'

The pharmacist gave his friend an embarrassed look. Wen Shou-fang replied diffidently, 'As a matter of fact, Your Honour, both of us took part in a banquet, held in the largest house in the Willow Quarter last night. Later we ah . . . retired upstairs, with ah . . . company. We went home a few hours after midnight.'

'I had a brief nap at home,' Yuan Kai added, 'then changed into hunting-dress and went to the tribunal to fetch Your Honour for our duck-hunt.'

'I see,' Judge Dee said. 'I am glad you told me, it saves me unnecessary work.'

'This lotus pond is really very attractive,' Wen said, looking relieved. While they were conducting the judge to the gate, he added: 'Unfortunately such ponds are usually infested with frogs.'

'They make an infernal noise at times,' Yuan Kai remarked as he opened the gate for Judge Dee.

The judge mounted his horse, and rode back to the tribunal.

The headman came to meet him in the courtyard and reported

81

that in the side hall everything was ready for the autopsy. Judge Dee went first to his private office. While the clerk was pouring him a cup of hot tea the judge wrote a brief note to Ma Joong, instructing him to question the two courtesans Yuan Kai and Wen Shou-fang had slept with the night before. He thought a moment, then added: 'Verify also whether the servant of the Mengs passed last night in his father's house.' He sealed the note and ordered the clerk to have it delivered to Ma Joong immediately. Then Judge Dee quickly munched a few dry cakes, and went to the side hall where the coroner and his two assistants were waiting for him.

The autopsy brought to light nothing new: the poet had been in good health; death had been caused by a dagger thrust that had penetrated the heart. The judge ordered the headman to have the body placed in a temporary coffin, pending final instructions as to the time and place of burial. He returned to his private office and set to work on the official papers that had come in, assisted by the senior clerk of the tribunal.

It was nearly noon when Ma Joong came back. After the judge had sent the clerk away, Ma Joong seated himself opposite Judge Dee's desk, twirled his short moustache and began with a smug smile, 'Peach Blossom was already up and about, sir! She was just making her toilet when I knocked. Last night had been her evening off, so she had gone to bed early. She was looking more charming than ever, I . . .'

'Yes, yes, come to your point!' the judge cut him short peevishly. Part of his stratagem had apparently miscarried. 'She must have told you quite a lot,' he continued, 'since you were gone nearly all morning.'

Ma Joong gave him a reproachful look. He said earnestly, 'One has to handle those girls carefully, sir. We had breakfast together, and I gradually brought her round to the subject of Mrs Meng. Her professional name was Agate, her real name Shih Mei-lan; she's a farmer's daughter from up north. Three years ago, when the big drought had caused famine and the people were dying like rats, her father sold her to a procurer, and he in turn sold her to the house where Peach Blossom is working. She was a pleasant, cheerful girl. The owner of the house confirmed that

82

Yuan Kai had sought Agate's favours, and that she had refused. He thinks she did so only in order to raise her price, for she seemed rather sorry when the pharmacist didn't insist but found himself another playmate. With Wen Shou-fang it was a little different. Wen is a rather shy fellow; when Agate didn't respond to his first overtures, he didn't try again but confined himself to worshipping her from a distance. Then Meng Lan met her, and bought her then and there. But Peach Blossom thinks that Wen is still very fond of Agate, he often talks about her with the other girls and recently said again that Agate had deserved a better husband than that grumpy old poetaster. I also found out that Agate has a younger brother, called Shih Ming, and that he is a really bad egg. He is a drinker and gambler, who followed his sister out here and used to live off her earnings. He disappeared about a year ago, just before Meng Lan married her. But last week he suddenly turned up in the quarter and asked after his sister. When the owner told him that Meng Lan had bought and married her, Shih Ming went at once to their country house. Later Meng's servant told people that Shih Ming had quarrelled with the poet; he hadn't understood what it was all about, but it had something to do with money. Mrs Meng cried bitterly, and Shih Ming left in a rage. He hasn't been seen since.'

Ma Joong paused, but Judge Dee made no comment. He slowly sipped his tea, his bushy eyebrows knitted in a deep frown. Suddenly he asked: 'Did Meng's servant go out last night?'

'No, sir. I questioned his father, the old gardener and also their neighbours. The youngster came home directly after dinner, fell down on the bed he shares with two brothers, and lay snoring there till daybreak. And that reminds me of your second point, sir. I found that Yuan Kai stayed last night with Peony, a friend of Peach Blossom. They went up to her room at midnight, and Yuan left the house two hours later, on foot—in order to enjoy the moonlight, he said. Wen Shou-fang stayed with a girl called Carnation, a comely wench, though she was in a bit of a sullen mood this morning. It seems that Wen had drunk too much during the banquet, and when he was up in Carnation's room he laid himself down on the bed and passed out. Carnation tried to rouse him in vain, went over to the girls in the next room for a card game and forgot all about him. He came to life three hours later, but to Carnation's disappointment he had such a hangover that he went straight home, also on foot. He preferred walking to sitting in a sedan chair, because he hoped the fresh air would clear his brain—so he said. That's all, sir. I think that Shih Ming is our man. By marrying his sister, Meng Lan took Shih Ming's rice-bowl away from him, so to speak. Shall I tell the headman to institute a search for Shih Ming? I have a good description of him.'

'Do that,' Judge Dee said. 'You can go now and have your noon rice, I won't need you until tonight.'

'Then I'll have a little nap,' Ma Joong said with satisfaction. 'I had quite a strenuous morning. What with the duck-hunt and everything.'

'I don't doubt it!' the judge said dryly.

When Ma Joong had taken his leave Judge Dee went upstairs to the marble terrace that overlooked the lake. He sat down in a large armchair, and had his noon rice served there. He didn't feel like going to his private residence at the back of the tribunal; preoccupied as he was with the murder case, he wouldn't be pleasant company for his family. When he had finished his meal he pulled the armchair into a shadowy corner on the terrace. But just as he was preparing himself for a brief nap, a messenger came up and handed him a long report from Sergeant Hoong. The sergeant wrote that the investigation in the western part of the district revealed that the attack on the treasury messenger had been perpetrated by a band of six ruffians. After they had beaten the man unconscious and taken the package with the gold bars, they coolly proceeded to an inn near the district boundary, and there they had a good meal. Then a stranger arrived; he kept his neckcloth over his nose and mouth, and the people of the inn had never seen him before. The leader of the robbers handed him a package, and then they all left in the direction of the forests of the neighbouring district. Later the body of the stranger had been found in a ditch, not far from the inn. He was recognized by his dress; his face had been beaten to pulp. The local coroner was an experienced man; he examined the contents of the dead man's stomach, and discovered traces of a strong drug. The package with the gold bars had, of course, disappeared. 'Thus the attack on the treasury messenger was carefully planned,' the sergeant wrote in conclusion, 'and by someone who has remained behind the scenes. He had his accomplice hire the ruffians to do the rough work, then sent that same accomplice to the inn to collect the booty. He himself followed the accomplice, drugged him and beat him to death, either because he wanted to eliminate a possible witness against him, or because he didn't want to pay him his share. In order to trace the criminal behind this affair we'll have to ask for the co-operation of Your Honour's colleague in the neighbouring district. I respectfully request Your Honour to proceed here so as to conduct the investigation personally.'

Judge Dee slowly rolled up the report. The sergeant was right, he ought to go there at once. But the poet's murder needed his attention too. Both Yuan Kai and Wen Shou-fang had had the opportunity, but neither of them seemed to have a motive. Mrs Meng's brother did indeed have a motive, but if he had done the deed he would doubtless have fled to some distant place by now. With a sigh he leaned back in his chair, pensively stroking his beard. Before he knew it he was sound asleep.

When he woke up he noticed to his annoyance that he had slept too long; dusk was already falling. Ma Joong and the headman were standing by the balustrade. The latter reported that the hue and cry was out for Shih Ming, but that as yet no trace of him had been found.

Judge Dee gave Ma Joong the sergeant's report, saying, 'You'd better read this carefully. Then you can make the necessary preparations for travelling to the west boundary of our district, for we shall go there early tomorrow morning. Among the incoming mail was a letter from the Treasury in the capital, ordering me to report without delay on the robbery. A missing string of coppers causes them sleepless nights, let alone a dozen good gold bars!'

The judge went downstairs and drafted in his private office a preliminary report to the Treasury. Then he had his evening meal served on his desk. He hardly tasted what he ate, his thoughts were elsewhere. Laying down his chopsticks, he reflected with a sigh that it was most unfortunate that the two crimes should have occurred at approximately the same time. Suddenly he set down his tea cup. He got up and started to pace the floor. He thought he had found the explanation of the missing wine cup. He would have to verify this at once. He stepped up to the window and looked at the courtyard outside. When he saw that there was no one about, he quickly crossed over to the side gate and left the tribunal unnoticed.

In the street he pulled his neckcloth up over the lower half of his face, and on the corner rented a small sedan chair. He paid the bearers off in front of the largest house in the Willow Quarter. Confused sounds of singing and laughter came from the brilliantly lit windows; apparently a gay banquet was already in progress there. Judge Dee quickly walked on and started along the path leading to Meng Lan's country house.

When he was approaching the garden gate he noticed that it was very quiet here; the trees cut off the noise from the Willow Quarter. He softly pushed the gate open and studied the garden. The moonlight shone on the lotus pond, the house at the back of the garden was completely dark. Judge Dee walked around the pond, then stooped and picked up a stone. He threw it into the pond. Immediately the frogs started to croak in chorus. With a satisfied smile Judge Dee went on to the door, again pulling his neckcloth up over his mouth and nose. Standing in the shadow of the porch, he knocked.

A light appeared behind the window. Then the door opened and he heard Mrs Meng's voice whispering, 'Come inside, quick!'

She was standing in the doorway, her torso naked. She only wore a thin loin-cloth, and her hair was hanging loose. When the judge let the neckcloth drop from his face she uttered a smothered cry.

'I am not the one you were expecting,' he said coldly, 'but I'll come in anyway.' He stepped inside, shut the door behind him and continued sternly to the cowering woman, 'Who were you waiting for?'

Her lips moved but no sound came forth.

'Speak up!' Judge Dee barked.

Clutching the loin-cloth round her waist she stammered, 'I wasn't waiting for anyone. I was awakened by the noise of the

SHE WAS STANDING IN THE DOORWAY, HER TORSO NAKED

frogs, and feared there was an intruder. So I came to have a look and . . .'

'And asked the intruder to come inside quickly! If you must lie, you'd better be more clever about it! Show me your bedroom where you were waiting for your lover!'

Silently she took the candle from the table, and led the judge to a small side room. It only contained a narrow plank-bed, covered by a thin reed mat. The judge quickly stepped up to the bed and felt the mat. It was still warm from her body. Righting himself, he asked sharply: 'Do you always sleep here?'

'No, Your Honour, this is the servant's room, the boy uses it for his afternoon nap. My bedroom is over on the other side of the hall we passed just now.'

'Take me there!'

When she had crossed the hall and shown the judge into the large bedroom he took the candle from her and quickly looked the room over. There was a dressing-table with a bamboo chair, four clothes-boxes, and a large bedstead. Judge Dee pulled the bedcurtains aside. He saw that the thick bedmat of soft reed had been rolled up, and that the pillows had been stored away in the recess in the back wall. He turned round to her and said angrily, 'I don't care where you were going to sleep with your lover, I only want to know his name. Speak up!'

She didn't answer, she only gave him a sidelong glance. Then her loin-cloth slipped down to the floor and she stood there stark naked. Covering herself with her hands, she looked coyly at him.

Judge Dee turned away. 'Those silly tricks bore me,' he said coldly. 'Get dressed at once, you'll come with me to the tribunal and pass the night in jail. Tomorrow I shall interrogate you in court, if necessary under torture.'

She silently opened a clothes-box and started to dress. The judge went to the hall and sat down there. He reflected that she was prepared to go a long way to shield her lover. Then he shrugged. Since she was a former courtesan, it wasn't really such a very long way. When she came in, fully dressed, he motioned her to follow him.

They met the night watch at the entrance of the Willow Quarter. The judge told their leader to take Mrs Meng in a sedan chair to the tribunal, and hand her to the warden of the jail. He was also to send four of his men to the dead poet's house, they were to hide in the hall and arrest anyone who knocked. Then Judge Dee walked back at a leisurely pace, deep in thought.

Passing the gatehouse of the tribunal, he saw Ma Joong sitting in the guardroom talking with the soldiers. He took his lieutenant to his private office. When he had told him what had happened in the country house, Ma Joong shook his head sadly and said, 'So she had a secret lover, and it was he who killed her husband. Well, that means that the case is practically solved. With some further persuasion, she'll come across with the fellow's name.'

Judge Dee took a sip from his tea, then said slowly, 'There are a few points that worry me, though. There's a definite connection between Meng's murder and the attack on the treasury messenger, but I haven't the faintest idea what it means. However, I want your opinion on two other points. First, how could Mrs Meng conduct a secret love affair? She and her husband practically never went out, and the few guests they received came during the day. Second, I verified that she was sleeping tonight in the servant's room, on a narrow plank-bed. Why didn't she prepare to receive her lover in the bedroom, where there is a large and comfortable bedstead? Deference to her dead husband couldn't have prevented her from that, if she had been merrily deceiving him behind his back! I know, of course, that lovers don't care much about comfort, but even so, that hard, narrow plank-bed . . .'

'Well,' Ma Joong said with a grin, 'as regards the first point, if a woman is determined on having her little games, you can be dead sure that she'll somehow manage to find ways and means. Perhaps it was that servant of theirs she was playing around with, and then her private pleasures had nothing to do with the murder. As to the second point, I have often enough slept on a plank-bed, but I confess I never thought of sharing it. I'll gladly go to the Willow Quarter, though, and make inquiries about its special advantages if any.' He looked hopefully at the judge.

Judge Dee was staring at him, but his thoughts seemed to be elsewhere. Slowly tugging at his moustache, he remained silent for some time. Suddenly the judge smiled. 'Yes,' he said, 'we might try that.' Ma Joong looked pleased. But his face fell as Judge Dee continued briskly, 'Go at once to the Inn of the Red Carp, behind the fishmarket. Tell the head of the beggars there to get you half a dozen beggars who frequent the vicinity of the Willow Quarter, and bring those fellows here. Tell the head of the guild that I want to interrogate them about important new facts that have come to light regarding the murder of the poet Meng Lan. Make no secret of it. On the contrary, see to it that everybody knows I am summoning these beggars, and for what purpose. Get going!'

As Ma Joong remained sitting there, looking dumbfounded at the judge, he added, 'If my scheme succeeds, I'll have solved both Meng's murder and the robbery of the gold bars. Do your best!'

Ma Joong got up and hurried outside.

When Ma Joong came back to Judge Dee's private office herding four ragged beggars he saw on the side table large platters with cakes and sweetmeats, and a few jugs of wine.

Judge Dee put the frightened men at their ease with some friendly words of greeting, then told them to taste the food and have a cup of wine. As the astonished beggars shuffled up to the table looking hungrily at the repast, Judge Dee took Ma Joong apart and said in a low voice:

'Go to the guardroom and select three good men from among the constables. You wait with them at the gate. In an hour or so I'll send the four beggars away. Each of them must be secretly followed. Arrest any person who accosts any one of them and bring him here, together with the beggar he addressed!'

Then he turned to the beggars, and encouraged them to partake freely of the food and wine. The perplexed vagabonds hesitated long before they fell to, but then the platters and cups were empty in an amazingly brief time. Their leader, a one-eyed scoundrel, wiped his hands on his greasy beard, then muttered resignedly to his companions, 'Now he'll have our heads chopped off. But I must say that it was a generous last meal.'

To their amazement, however, Judge Dee made them sit down on tabourets in front of his desk. He questioned each of them about the place he came from, his age, his family and many other innocent details. When the beggars found that he didn't touch upon any awkward subjects, they began to talk more freely, and soon an hour had passed.

Judge Dee rose, thanked them for their co-operation and told them they could go. Then he began to pace the floor, his hands clasped behind his back.

Sooner than he had expected there was a knock. Ma Joong came in, dragging the one-eyed beggar along.

'He gave me the silver piece before I knew what was happening, Excellency!' the old man whined. 'I swear I didn't pick his pocket!'

'I know you didn't,' Judge Dee said. 'Don't worry, you can keep that silver piece. Just tell me what he said to you.'

'He comes up to me when I am rounding the street corner, Excellency, and presses that silver piece into my hand. He says: "Come with me, you'll get another one if you tell me what that judge asked you and your friends." I swear that's the truth, Excellency!'

'Good! You can go. Don't spend the money on wine and gambling!' As the beggar scurried away the judge said to Ma Joong: 'Bring the prisoner!'

The pharmacist Yuan Kai started to protest loudly as soon as he was inside. 'A prominent citizen arrested like a common criminal! I demand to know . . .'

'And I demand to know,' Judge Dee interrupted him coldly, 'why you were lying in wait for that beggar, and why you questioned him.'

'Of course I am deeply interested in the progress of the investigation, Your Honour! I was eager to know whether . . .'

'Whether I had found a clue leading to you which you had overlooked,' the judge completed the sentence for him. 'Yuan Kai, you murdered the poet Meng Lan, and also Shih Ming, whom you used to contact the ruffians that robbed the treasury messenger. Confess your crimes!'

Yuan Kai's face had turned pale. But he had his voice well under control when he asked sharply: 'I suppose Your Honour has good grounds for proffering such grave accusations?'

'I have. Mrs Meng stated that they never received visitors at night. She also stated that the frogs in the lotus pond never croak during the day. Yet you remarked on the noise they make—sometimes. That suggested that you had been there at night. Further, Meng had been drinking wine with his murderer, who left his own cup on the table, but took away Meng's special cup. That, together with Meng's calm face, told me that he had been drugged before he was killed, and that the murderer had taken his victim's cup away with him because he feared that it would still smell after the drug, even if he washed it there in the pond. Now the accomplice of the criminal who organized the attack on the treasury messenger was also drugged before he was killed. This suggested that both crimes were committed by one and the same person. It made me suspect you, because as a pharmacist you know all about drugs, and because you had the opportunity to kill Meng Lan after you had left the Willow Quarter. I also remembered that we hadn't done too well on our duck-hunt this morning—we caught nothing. Although an expert hunter like you led our party. You were in bad form, because you had quite a strenuous night behind you. But by teaching me the method of duck-hunting with a decoy, you suggested to me a simple means for verifying my suspicions. Tonight I used the beggars as a decoy, and I caught you.'

'And my motive?' Yuan Kai asked slowly.

'Some facts that are no concern of yours made me discover that Mrs Meng had been expecting her brother Shih Ming to visit her secretly at night, and that proved that she knew that he had committed some crime. When Shih Ming visited his sister and his brother-in-law last week, and when they refused to give him money, he became angry and boasted that you had enlisted his help in an affair that would bring in a lot of money. Meng and his wife knew that Shih Ming was no good, so when they heard about the attack on the treasury messenger, and when Shih Ming didn't show up, they concluded it must be the affair Shih Ming had alluded to. Meng Lan was an honest man, and he taxed you with the robbery—there was your motive. Mrs Meng wanted to shield her brother, but when presently she learns that it was you who murdered her husband, and also her brother, she'll speak, and her testimony will conclude the case against you, Yuan Kai.'

The pharmacist looked down; he was breathing heavily. Judge Dee went on, 'I shall apologize to Mrs Meng. The unfortunate profession she exercised hasn't affected her staunch character. She was genuinely fond of her husband, and although she knew that her brother was a good-for-nothing, she was prepared to be flogged in the tribunal for contempt of court, rather than give him away. Well, she'll soon be a rich woman, for half of your property shall be assigned to her, as blood-money for her husband's murder. And doubtless Wen Shou-fang will in due time ask her to marry him, for he is still deeply in love with her. As to you, Yuan Kai, you are a foul murderer, and your head will fall on the execution ground.'

Suddenly Yuan looked up. He said in a toneless voice, 'It was that accursed frog that did for me! I killed the creature, and kicked it into the pond. That set the other frogs going.' Then he added bitterly : 'And, fool that I was, I said frogs can't talk !'

'They can,' Judge Dee said soberly. 'And they did.'

THE TWO BEGGARS

This story explains why Judge Dee was late for his family dinner on the Feast of Lanterns. This feast is the concluding phase of the protracted New Year's celebrations; in the evening an intimate family dinner is held, and the ladies of the household consult the oracle on what the New Year has in store for them. The scene of this story is laid in Poo-yang, well-known to readers of the novel The Chinese Bell Murders. *Chapter IX of that book mentions Magistrate Lo, Judge Dee's volatile colleague in the neighbouring district of Chin-hwa, who now figures in this tale about the sad fate that befell two beggars.*

When the last visitor had left, Judge Dee leaned back in his chair with a sigh of relief. With tired eyes he looked out over his back garden where in the gathering dusk his three small sons were playing among the shrubbery. They were suspending lighted lanterns on the branches, painted with the images of the Eight Genii.

It was the fifteenth day of the first month, the Feast of Lanterns. People were hanging gaily painted lanterns of all shapes and sizes in and outside their houses, transforming the entire city into a riot of garish colours. From the other side of the garden wall the judge heard the laughter of people strolling in the park.

All through the afternoon the notables of Poo-yang, the prosperous district where Judge Dee had now been serving one year as magistrate, had been coming to his residence at the back of the tribunal compound to offer him their congratulations on this auspicious day. He pushed his winged judge's cap back from his forehead and passed his hand over his face. He was not accustomed to drinking so much wine in the daytime; he felt slightly sick. Leaning forward, he took a large white rose from the bowl on the tea-table, for its scent is supposed to counteract the effects of alcohol. Inhaling deeply the flower's fresh fragrance, the judge reflected that his last visitor, Ling, the master of the goldsmiths' guild, had really overstayed his welcome, had seemed glued to his chair. And Judge Dee had to change and refresh himself before going to his women's quarters, where his three wives were now supervising the preparations for the festive family dinner.

Excited children's voices rang out from the garden. The judge looked round and saw that his two eldest boys were struggling to get hold of a large coloured lantern.

'Better come inside now and have your bath!' Judge Dee called out over to them.

'Ah-kuei wants that nice lantern made by Big Sister and me all for himself!' his eldest son shouted indignantly.

The judge was going to repeat his command, but out of the corner of his eye he saw the door in the back of the hall open. Sergeant Hoong, his confidential adviser, came shuffling inside. Noticing how wan and tired the old man looked, Judge Dee said quickly, 'Take a seat and have a cup of tea, Hoong! I am sorry I had to leave all the routine business of the tribunal to you today. I had to go over to the chancery and do some work after my guests had left, but Master Ling was more talkative than ever. He took his leave only a few moments ago.'

'There was nothing of special importance, Your Honour,' Sergeant Hoong said, as he poured the judge and himself a cup of tea. 'My only difficulty was to keep the clerks with their noses to the grindstone. Today's festive spirit had got hold of them!'

Hoong sat down and sipped his tea, carefully holding up his ragged grey moustache with his left thumb.

'Well, the Feast of Lanterns is on,' the judge said, putting the white rose back on the table.' As long as no urgent cases are reported, we can afford to be a little less strict for once.'

Sergeant Hoong nodded. 'The warden of the north quarter came to the chancery just before noon and reported an accident, sir. An old beggar fell into a deep drain, in a back street not far from Master Ling's residence. His head hit a sharp stone at the bottom, and he died. Our coroner performed the autopsy and signed the certificate of accidental death. The poor wretch was clad only in a tattered gown, he hadn't even a cap on his head, and his greying hair was hanging loose. He was a cripple. He must have stumbled into the drain going out at dawn for his morning rounds. Sheng Pa, the head of the beggars, couldn't identify him. Poor fellow must have come to the city from up-country expecting good earnings here during the feast. If nobody comes to claim the corpse, we'll have it burned tomorrow.'

Judge Dee looked round at his eldest son, who was moving an armchair among the pillars that lined the open front of the hall. The judge snapped: 'Stop fiddling around with that chair, and do as I told you! All three of you!'

'Yes, sir!' the three boys shouted in chorus.

While they were rushing away, Judge Dee said to Hoong: 'Tell the warden to have the drain covered up properly, and give him a good talking to! Those fellows are supposed to see to it that the streets in their quarter are kept in good repair. By the way, we expect you to join our small family dinner tonight, Hoong!'

The old man bowed with a gratified smile.

'I'll go now to the chancery and lock up, sir! I'll present myself at Your Honour's residence again in half an hour.'

After the sergeant had left, Judge Dee reflected that he ought to go too and change from his ceremonial robe of stiff green brocade into a comfortable house-gown. But he felt loath to leave the quiet atmosphere of the now empty hall, and thought he might as well have one more cup of tea. In the park outside it had grown quiet too; people had gone home for the evening rice. Later they would swarm out into the street again, to admire the display of lanterns and have drinking bouts in the roadside wine-houses. Putting his cup down, Judge Dee reflected that perhaps he shouldn't have given Ma Joong and his two other lieutenants the night off, for later in the evening there might be brawls in the brothel district. He must remember to tell the headman of the constables to double the night watch.

He stretched his hand out again for his teacup. Suddenly he checked himself. He stared fixedly at the shadows at the back of the hall. A tall old man had come in. He seemed to be clad in a tattered robe, his head with the long flowing hair was bare. Silently he limped across the hall, supporting himself on a crooked staff. He didn't seem to notice the judge, but went straight past with bent head.

96

Judge Dee was going to shout and ask what he meant by coming in unannounced, but the words were never spoken. The judge froze in sudden horror. The old man seemed to flit right through the large cupboard, then stepped down noiselessly into the garden.

The judge jumped up and ran to the garden steps. 'Come back, you !' he shouted angrily.

There was no answer.

Judge Dee stepped down into the moonlit garden. Nobody was there. He quickly searched the low shrubbery along the wall, but found nothing. And the small garden gate to the park outside was securely locked and barred as usual.

The judge remained standing there. Shivering involuntarily, he pulled his robe closer to his body. He had seen the ghost of the dead beggar.

After a while he took hold of himself. He turned round abruptly, went back up to the hall and entered the dim corridor leading to the front of his private residence. He returned absent-mindedly the respectful greeting of his doorman, who was lighting two brightly coloured lanterns at the gate, then crossed the central courtyard of the tribunal compound and walked straight to the chancery.

The clerks had gone home already; only Sergeant Hoong was there, sorting out a pile of papers on his desk by the light of a single candle. He looked up astonished as he saw the judge come in.

'I thought that I might as well have a look at that dead beggar after all,' Judge Dee said casually.

Hoong quickly lit a new candle. He led the judge through the dark, deserted corridors to the jail at the back of the courtroom. In the side hall a thin form was lying on a deal table, covered by a reed mat.

Judge Dee took the candle from Hoong, and motioned him to remove the mat. Raising the candle, the judge stared at the lifeless, haggard face. It was deeply lined, and the cheeks were hollow, but it lacked the coarse features one would expect in a beggar. He seemed about fifty; his long, tousled hair was streaked with grey. The thin lips under the short moustache were distorted in a repulsive death grimace. He wore no beard.

The judge pulled open the lower part of the tattered, patched gown. Pointing at the misshapen left leg, he remarked, 'He must have broken his knee once, and it was badly set. He must have walked with a pronounced limp.'

Sergeant Hoong picked up a long crooked staff standing in the corner and said, 'Since he was quite tall, he supported himself on this crutch. It was found by his side, at the bottom of the drain.'

Judge Dee nodded. He tried to raise the left arm of the corpse, but it was quite stiff. Stooping, he scrutinized the hand, then righting himself, he said, 'Look at this, Hoong! These soft hands without any callouses, the long, well-tended fingernails! Turn the body over!'

When the sergeant had rolled the stiff corpse over on its face Judge Dee studied the gaping wound at the back of the skull. After a while he handed the candle to Hoong, and taking a paper handkerchief from his sleeve, he used it to carefully brush aside the matted grey hair, which was clotted with dried blood. He then examined the handkerchief under the candle. Showing it to Hoong, he said curtly: 'Do you see this fine sand and white grit? You wouldn't expect to find that at the bottom of a drain, would you?'

Sergeant Hoong shook his head perplexedly. He replied slowly, 'No, sir. Slime and mud rather, I'd say.'

Judge Dee walked over to the other end of the table and looked at the bare feet. They were white, and the soles were soft. Turning to the sergeant, he said gravely, 'I fear that our coroner's thoughts were on tonight's feast rather than on his duties when he performed the post-mortem. This man wasn't a beggar, and he didn't fall accidentally into the drain. He was thrown into it when he was dead already. By the person who murdered him.'

Sergeant Hoong nodded, ruefully pulling at his short grey beard. 'Yes, the murderer must have stripped him, and put him in that beggar's gown. It should have struck me at once that the man was naked under that tattered robe. Even a poor beggar would have been wearing something underneath; the evenings are still rather chilly.' Looking again at the gaping wound, he asked: 'Do you think the head was bashed in with a heavy club, sir?'

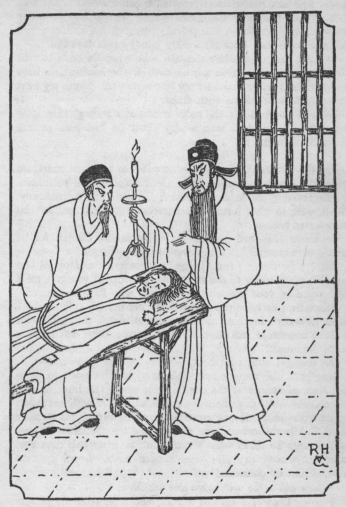

RAISING THE CANDLE, THE JUDGE STARED AT THE LIFELESS,
HAGGARD FACE

'Perhaps,' Judge Dee replied. He smoothed down his long, black beard. 'Has any person been reported missing recently?'

'Yes, Your Honour! Guildmaster Ling sent a note yesterday stating that Mr Wang, the private tutor of his children, had failed to come back from his weekly holiday two days ago.'

'Strange that Ling didn't mention that when he came to visit me just now!' Judge Dee muttered. 'Tell the headman to have my palankeen ready! And let my house steward inform my First Lady not to wait for me with dinner!'

After Hoong had left, the judge remained standing there, looking down at the dead man whose ghost he had seen passing through the hall.

The old guildmaster came rushing out into his front courtyard when the bearers deposited Judge Dee's large official palankeen. While assisting the judge to descend, Ling inquired boisterously, 'Well, well, to what fortunate occurrence am I indebted for this unexpected honour?'

Evidently Ling had just left a festive family dinner, for he reeked of wine and his words were slightly slurred.

'Hardly fortunate, I fear,' Judge Dee remarked, as Ling led him and Sergeant Hoong to the reception hall. 'Could you give me a description of your house tutor, the one who has disappeared?'

'Heavens, I do hope the fellow didn't get himself into trouble! Well, he wasn't anything special to look at. A tall thin man, with a short moustache, no beard. Walked with a limp, left leg was badly deformed.'

'He has met with a fatal accident,' Judge Dee said evenly.

Ling gave him a quick look, then motioned his guest to sit in the place of honour at the central table under the huge lantern of coloured silk hung there for the feast. He himself sat down opposite the judge. Hoong remained standing behind his master's chair. While the steward was pouring the tea, Guildmaster Ling said slowly, 'So that's why Wang didn't turn up two days ago, after his weekly day off!' The sudden news seemed to have sobered him up considerably.

'Where did he go to?' Judge Dee asked.

'Heaven knows! I am not a man who pries into the private

affairs of his household staff. Wang had every Thursday off; he would leave here Wednesday night before dinner, and return Thursday evening, also at dinner time. That's all I know, and all I need to know, if I may say so, sir!'

'How long had he been with you?'

'About one year. Came from the capital with an introduction from a well-known goldsmith there. Since I needed a tutor to teach my grandsons, I engaged him. Found him a quiet, decent fellow. Quite competent too.'

'Do you know why he chose to leave the capital and seek employment here in Poo-yang? Did he have any family here?'

'I don't know,' Ling replied crossly. 'It was not my habit to discuss with him anything except the progress of my grandchildren.'

'Call your house steward!'

The guildmaster turned round in his chair and beckoned the steward who was hovering about in the back of the spacious hall.

When he had come up to the table and made his obeisance Judge Dee said to him, 'Mr Wang has met with an accident and the tribunal must inform the next of kin. You know the address of his relatives here, I suppose?'

The steward cast an uneasy glance at his master. He stammered 'He . . . as far as I know Mr Wang didn't have any relative living here in Poo-yang, Your Honour.'

'Where did he go then for his weekly holidays?'

'He never told me, sir. I suppose he went to see a friend or something.' Seeing Judge Dee's sceptical expression, he quickly went on, 'Mr Wang was a taciturn man, Your Honour, and he always evaded questions about his private affairs. He liked to be alone. He spent his spare hours in the small room he has in the back yard of this residence. His only recreation was brief walks in our garden.'

'Didn't he receive or send any letters?'

'Not that I know of, sir.' The steward hesitated a moment 'From some chance remarks of his about his former life in the capital I gathered that his wife had left him. It seemed that she was of a very jealous disposition.' He gave his employer an anxious glance. As he saw that Ling was staring ahead and didn't seem to be listening, he went on with more self-assurance: 'Mr Wang had no private means at all, sir, and he was very parsimonious. He hardly spent one cent of his salary, never even took a sedan chair when he went out on his day off. But he must have been a wealthy man once, I could tell that from some small mannerisms of his. I think that he was even an official once, for sometimes when caught off guard he would address me in rather an authoritative tone. I understand he lost everything, his money and his official position. Didn't seem to mind, though. Once he said to me: "Money is of no use if you don't enjoy life spending it; and when your money is spent, official life has lost its glamour." Rather a frivolous remark coming from such a learned gentleman, I thought, sir—if I may make so bold, sir.'

Ling glared at him and said with a sneer, 'You seem to find time hanging heavily on your hands in this household! Gossiping instead of supervising the servants!'

'Let the man speak!' the judge snapped at Ling. And to the steward: 'Was there absolutely no clue as to where Mr Wang used to go on his days off? You must know; you saw him go in and out, didn't you?'

The steward frowned. Then he replied, 'Well, it did strike me that Mr Wang always seemed happy when he went, but when he came back he was usually rather depressed. He had melancholy moods at times. Never interfered with his teaching, though, sir. He was always ready to answer difficult questions, the young miss said the other day.'

'You stated that Wang only taught your grandchildren,' the judge said sharply to Ling. 'Now it appears that he also taught your daughter!'

The guildmaster gave his steward a furious look. He moistened his lips, then replied curtly, 'He did. Until she was married, two months ago.'

'I see.' Judge Dee rose from his chair and told the steward: 'Show me Mr Wang's room!' He motioned to Sergeant Hoong to follow him. As Ling made a move to join them, the judge said: 'Your presence is not required.'

The steward led the judge and Hoong through a maze of corridors to the back yard of the extensive compound. He unlocked a narrow door, lifted the candle and showed them a small, poorly furnished room. There was only a bamboo couch, a simple writing-desk with a straight-backed chair, a bamboo rack with a few books and a black-leather clothes-box. The walls were covered with long strips of paper, bearing ink-sketches of orchids, done with considerable skill. Following Judge Dee's glance, the steward said:

'That was Mr Wang's only hobby, sir. He loved orchids, knew everything about tending them.'

'Didn't he have a few potted orchids about?' the judge asked.

'No, sir. I don't think he could afford to buy them—they are quite expensive, sir!'

Judge Dee nodded. He picked up a few of the dog-eared volumes from the book rack and glanced through them. It was romantic poetry, in cheap editions. Then he opened the clothes-box. It was stuffed with men's garments, worn threadbare. but of good quality. The cash box at the bottom of the box contained only some small change. The judge turned to the desk. The drawer had no lock. Inside were the usual writing materials, but no money and not a scrap of inscribed paper, not even a receipted bill. He slammed the drawer shut and angrily asked the steward, 'Who has rifled this room during Mr Wang's absence?'

'Nobody has been here, Your Honour!' the frightened steward stammered. 'Mr Wang always locked the door when he went out, and I have the only spare key.'

'You yourself told me that Wang didn't spend a cent, didn't you? What has happened to his savings over the past year? There's only some small change here!'

The steward shook his head in bewilderment. 'I really couldn't say, Your Honour! I am sure nobody came in here. And all the servants have been with us for years. There has never been any pilfering, I can assure you, sir!'

Judge Dee remained standing for a while by the desk. He stared at the paintings, slowly tugging at his moustache. Then he turned round and said: 'Take us back to the hall!'

While the steward was conducting them again through the winding corridors, Judge Dee remarked casually, 'This residence is situated in a nice, quiet neighbourhood.'

'Oh yes, indeed, sir, very quiet and respectable!'

'It's exactly in such a nice, respectable neighbourhood that one finds the better houses of assignation,' the judge remarked dryly. 'Are there any near here?'

The steward seemed taken aback by this unexpected question. He cleared his throat and replied diffidently, 'Only one, sir, two streets away. It's kept by a Mrs Kwang—very high class, visited by the best people only, sir. Never any brawls or other trouble here, sir.'

'I am glad to hear that,' Judge Dee said.

Back in the reception hall he told the guildmaster that he would have to accompany him to the tribunal to make the formal identification of the dead man. While they were being carried out there in Judge Dee's palankeen, the guildmaster observed a surly silence.

After Ling had stated that the dead body was indeed that of his house tutor and filled out the necessary documents, Judge Dee let him go. Then he said to Sergeant Hoong, 'I'll now change into a more comfortable robe. In the meantime you tell our headman to stand by in the courtyard with two constables.'

Sergeant Hoong found the judge in his private office. He had changed into a simple robe of dark-grey cotton with a broad black sash, and he had placed a small black skull-cap on his head.

Hoong wanted to ask him where they were going, but seeing Judge Dee's preoccupied mien, he thought better of it and silently followed him out into the courtyard.

The headman and two constables sprang to attention when they saw the judge.

'Do you know the address of a house of assignation in the north quarter, close by Guildmaster Ling's residence?' Judge Dee asked.

'Certainly, Your Honour!' the headman answered officiously. 'That's Mrs Kwang's establishment. Properly licensed, and very high class, sir, only the best . . .'

'I know, I know!' the judge cut him short impatiently. 'We'll walk out there. You lead the way with your men!'

Now the streets were crowded again with people. They were milling around under the garlands of coloured lanterns that

104

spanned the streets and decorated the fronts of all the shops and restaurants. The headman and the two constables unceremoniously elbowed people aside, making way for the judge and Sergeant Hoong.

Even in the back street where Mrs Kwang lived there were many people about. When the headman had knocked and told the gatekeeper that the magistrate had arrived, the frightened old man quickly conducted the judge and Hoong to a luxuriously appointed waiting-room in the front court.

An elderly, sedately dressed maidservant placed a tea-set of exquisite antique porcelain on the table. Then a tall, handsome woman of about thirty came in, made a low bow and introduced herself as Mrs Kwang, a widow. She wore a straight, long-sleeved robe, simple in style but made of costly, dark-violet damask. She herself poured the tea for the judge, elegantly holding up with her left hand the trailing sleeve of the right. She remained standing in front of the judge, respectfully waiting for him to address her. Sergeant Hoong stood behind Judge Dee's chair, his arms folded in his wide sleeves.

Leisurely tasting the fragrant tea, Judge Dee noticed how quiet it was; all noise was kept out by the embroidered curtains and wall-hangings of heavy brocade. The faint scent of rare and very expensive incense floated in the air. All very high class indeed. He set down his cup and began, 'I disapprove of your trade, Mrs Kwang. I recognize, however, that it is a necessary evil. As long as you keep everything orderly and treat the girls well, I won't make any trouble for you. Tell me, how many girls have you working here?'

'Eight, Your Honour. All purchased in the regular manner, of course, mostly directly from their parents. Every three months the ledgers with their earnings are sent to the tribunal, for the assessment of my taxes. I trust that . . .'

'No, I have no complaints about that. But I am informed that one of the girls was bought out recently by a wealthy patron. Who is the fortunate girl?'

Mrs Kwang looked politely astonished. 'There must be some misunderstanding, Your Honour. All my girls here are still very young—the eldest is just nineteen—and haven't yet completed their training in music and dancing. They try hard to please, of course, but none of them has yet succeeded in captivating the favour of a wealthy patron so as to establish an ah . . . more permanent relationship.' She paused, then added primly, 'Although such a transaction means, of course, a very substantial monetary gain for me, I don't encourage it until a courtesan is well into her twenties, and in every respect worthy of attaining the crowning success of her career.'

'I see,' Judge Dee said. He thought ruefully that this information disposed effectively of his attractive theory. Now that his hunch had proved wrong, this case would necessitate a long investigation, beginning with the goldsmith in the capital who had introduced Wang to Guildmaster Ling. Suddenly another possibility flashed through his mind. Yes, he thought he could take the chance. Giving Mrs Kwang a stern look he said coldly:

'Don't prevaricate, Mrs Kwang! Besides the eight girls who are living here, you have established another in a house of her own. That's a serious offence, for your licence covers this house only.'

Mrs Kwang put a lock straight in her elaborate coiffure. The gesture made her long sleeve slip back, revealing her white, rounded forearm. Then she replied calmly:

'That information is only partly correct, Your Honour. I suppose it refers to Miss Liang, who lives in the next street. She is an accomplished courtesan from the capital, about thirty years old—her professional name is Rosedew. Since she was very popular in elegant circles in the capital, she saved a great deal of money and bought herself free, without, however, handing in her licence. She wanted to settle down, and came here to Poo-yang for a period of rest, and to have a leisurely look around for a suitable marriage partner. She's a very intelligent woman, sir; she knows that all those elegant, flighty young men in the capital don't go for permanent arrangements, so she wanted a steady, elderly man of some means and position. Only occasionally did she receive such selected clients here in my house. Your Honour will find the pertaining entries in a separate ledger, also duly submitted regularly for inspection. Since Miss Liang has kept her licence, and since the taxes on her earnings are paid . . .'

She let her voice trail off. Judge Dee was secretly very pleased, for he knew now that he had been on the right track after all. But he assumed an angry mien, hit his fist on the table and barked, 'So the man who is buying Rosedew out to marry her is being meanly deceived! For there is no redemption fee to be paid! Not one copper, neither to you nor to her former owner in the capital! Speak up! Weren't you and she going to share that fee, obtained from the unsuspecting patron under false pretences?'

At this Mrs Kwang lost her composure at last. She knelt down in front of Judge Dee's chair and repeatedly knocked her forehead on the floor. Looking up, she wailed, 'Please forgive this ignorant person, Excellency! The money has not yet been handed over. Her patron is an exalted person, Excellency, a colleague of Your Excellency, in fact, the magistrate of a district in this same region. If he should hear about this, he . . .'

She burst into tears.

Judge Dee turned round and gave Sergeant Hoong a significant look. That could be no one else but his amorous colleague of Chin-hwa, Magistrate Lo! He barked at Mrs Kwang: 'It was indeed Magistrate Lo who asked me to investigate. Tell me where Miss Liang lives; I shall interrogate her personally about this disgraceful affair!'

A short walk brought the judge and his men to the address in the next street that the tearful Mrs Kwang had given him.

Before knocking on the gate, the headman quickly looked up and down the street, then said, 'If I am not greatly mistaken, sir, the drain that beggar fell into is located right at the back of this house.'

'Good!' Judge Dee exclaimed. 'Here, I'll knock myself. You and your two men keep close to the wall while I go inside with the sergeant. Wait here till I call you!'

After repeated knocking the peephole grate in the gate opened and a woman's voice asked, 'Who is there?'

'I have a message from Magistrate Lo, for a Miss Rosedew,' Judge Dee said politely.

The door opened at once. A small woman dressed in a thin housecrobe of white silk asked the two men to enter. As she preceded them to the open hall in the front court, the judge noticed that despite her frail build she had an excellent figure.

When they were inside she gave her two visitors a curious look, then bade them seat themselves on the couch of carved rosewood. She said somewhat diffidently: 'I am indeed Rosedew. Who do I have the honour of . . .'

'We shan't take much of your time, Miss Liang,' the judge interrupted quickly. He looked her over. She had a finely chiselled mobile face, with expressive, almond-shaped eyes and a delicate small mouth—a woman of considerable intelligence and charm. Yet something didn't fit with his theory.

He surveyed the elegantly furnished hall. His eye fell on a high rack of polished bamboo in front of the side window. Each of its three superimposed shelves bore a row of orchid plants, potted in beautiful porcelain bowls. Their delicate fragrance pervaded the air. Pointing at the rack, he said: 'Magistrate Lo told me about your fine collection of orchids, Miss Liang. I am a great lover of them myself. Look, what a pity! The second one on the top shelf has wilted, it needs special treatment, I think. Could you get it down and show it to me?'

She gave him a doubtful look, but apparently decided that it was better to humour this queer friend of Magistrate Lo. She took a bamboo step-ladder from the corner, placed it in front of the rack, and nimbly climbed up, modestly gathering the thin robe round her shapely legs. When she was about to take the pot, Judge Dee suddenly stepped up close to the ladder and remarked casually:

'Mr Wang used to call you Orchid, didn't he, Miss Liang? So much more apposite than Rosedew, surely!' When Miss Liang stood motionless, looking down at the judge with eyes that were suddenly wide with fear, he added sharply: 'Mr Wang was standing exactly where I am standing now when you smashed the flower pot down on his head, wasn't he?'

She started to sway. Uttering a cry, she wildly groped for support. Judge Dee quickly steadied the ladder. Reaching up, he caught her round her waist and set her down on the floor. She clasped her hands to her heaving bosom and gasped: 'I don't . . Who are you?'

'I am the magistrate of Poo-yang,' the judge replied coldly. 'After you murdered Wang, you replaced the broken flower pot by a new one, and transplanted the orchid. That's why it's wilted, isn't it?'

'It's a lie!' she cried out. 'Wicked slander. I shall . . .'

'I have proof!' Judge Dee cut her short. 'A servant of the neighbours saw you dragging the dead body to the drain behind your house here. And I found in Wang's room a note of his, stating that he feared you would harm him, now that you had a wealthy patron who wanted to marry you.'

'The treacherous dog!' she shouted. 'He swore he didn't keep one scrap of paper relating to . . .' She suddenly stopped and angrily bit her red lips.

'I know everything,' the judge said evenly. 'Wang wanted more than his weekly visits. Thus he endangered your affair with Magistrate Lo, an affair that would not only bring in a lump sum of money for you and Mrs Kwang, but also set you up for life. Therefore you had to kill your lover.'

'Lover?' she screamed. 'Do you think I allowed that disgusting cripple ever to touch me here? It was bad enough to have to submit to his odious embraces before, when we were still in the capital!'

'Yet you allowed him to share your bed here,' Judge Dee remarked with disdain.

'You know where he slept? In the kitchen! I wouldn't have allowed him to come at all, but he made himself useful by answering my love letters for me, and he paid for and tended those orchids there, so that I would have flowers to wear in my hair. He also acted as doorman and brought tea and refreshments when one of my lovers was here. What else do you think I allowed him to come here for?'

'Since he had spent his entire fortune on you I thought perhaps . . .' Judge Dee said dryly.

'The damnable fool!' she burst out again. 'Even after I had told him that I was through with him, he kept on running after me, saying he couldn't live without seeing my face now and then —the cringing beggar! His ridiculous devotion spoilt my reputation. It was because of him that I had to leave the capital and

109

bury myself in this dreary place. And I, fool that I was, trusted that simpering wretch! Leaving a note accusing me! He's ruined me, the dirty traitor!'

Her beautiful face had changed into an evil mask. She stamped her small foot on the floor in impotent rage.

'No,' Judge Dee said in a tired voice, 'Wang didn't accuse you. What I said just now about that note wasn't true. Beyond a few paintings of orchids which he did when thinking of you, there wasn't one clue to you in his room. The poor, misguided man remained loyal to you, to his very end!' He clapped his hands. When the headman and the two constables had come rushing inside, he ordered: 'Put this woman in chains and lock her up in jail. She has confessed to a foul murder.' As the two constables grabbed her arms and the headman started to chain her, the judge said: 'Since there is not a single reason for clemency, you shall be beheaded on the execution ground.'

He turned round and left, followed by Sergeant Hoong. The woman's frantic cries were drowned by the loud shouts and laughter of a happy group of youngsters who came surging through the street, waving brightly coloured lanterns.

When they were back in the tribunal, Judge Dee took Hoong straight to his own residence. While walking with him to the back hall, he said, 'Let's just have one cup of tea before we go and join the dinner in my women's quarters.'

The two men sat down at the round table. The large lantern hanging from the eaves, and those among the shrubs in the garden had been extinguished. But the full moon lit up the hall with its eerie light.

Judge Dee quickly emptied his cup, then he sat back in his chair and began without further preliminaries:

'Before we went to see Guildmaster Ling, I knew only that the beggar was no beggar, and that he had been murdered elsewhere by having the back of his skull bashed in, probably with a flower pot—as suggested by the fine sand and white grit. Then, during our interview with Ling, I suspected for a moment that the guildmaster was involved in this crime. He hadn't said a word about Wang's disappearance when he came to visit me, and I thought it strange that later he didn't inquire what exactly had happened to Wang. But I soon realized that Ling is that unpleasant kind of person who doesn't take the slightest interest in his personnel, and that he was cross because I had interrupted his family party. What the steward told me about Wang brought to light a fairly clear pattern. The steward said that Wang's family life had been broken up because he squandered his wealth, and his mentioning Mrs Wang's jealousy pointed to another woman being involved. Thus I deducted that Wang had become deeply infatuated with a famous courtesan.'

'Why not with some decent girl or woman, or even with a common prostitute?' the sergeant objected.

'If it had been a decent woman, Wang would not have needed to spend his fortune on her; he could have divorced his wife and married his lady-love. And if she had been a common prostitute, he could have bought her out at a moderate price, and set her up in a small house of her own—all without sacrificing his wealth and his official position. No, I was certain that Wang's mistress must have been a famous courtesan in the capital, who could afford to squeeze a lover dry, then discard him and go on to the next. But I assumed that Wang refused to let himself be thrown away like a chewed-out piece of sugar cane, and that he made a nuisance of himself. That she fled from the capital and came to Poo-yang in order to start her game all over again. For it's well known that many wealthy merchants are living here in this district. I assumed that Wang had traced her here and had forced her to let him visit her regularly, threatening to expose her callous racket if she refused. Finally, that after she had caught my foolish colleague Lo, Wang began to blackmail her, and that therefore she had killed him.' He sighed, then added: 'We now know that it was quite different. Wang sacrificed everything he had for her, and even the pittance he received as tutor he spent on orchids for her. He was quite content to be allowed to see and talk to her every week, frustrating and humiliating as those few hours were. Sometimes, Hoong, a man's folly is engendered by such a deep and reckless passion that it lends him a kind of pathetic grandeur.'

Sergeant Hoong pensively pulled at his ragged grey moustache. After a while he asked, 'There are a great many courtesans here in Poo-yang. How did Your Honour know that Wang's mistress must belong to the house of Mrs Kwang? And why did it have to be his mistress who murdered him and not, for instance, another jealous lover?'

'Wang used to go there on foot. Since he was a cripple, this proved that she must live near to the guildmaster's house, and that led us to Mrs Kwang's establishment. I asked Mrs Kwang what courtesan had been recently bought out, because such an occurrence supplied the most plausible motive for the murder, namely that the courtesan had to get rid of an embarrassing former lover. Well, we know that Wang was indeed embarrassing her, but not by threatening to blackmail her or by any other wicked scheme. It was just his dog-like devotion that made her hate and despise him. As to the other possibilities you just mentioned, I had of course also reckoned with those. But if the murderer had been a man, he would have carried the body away to some distant spot, and he would also have been more thorough in his attempts at concealing his victim's identity. The fact that the attempt was confined to dressing the victim in a tattered beggar's gown, loosening his top-knot and mussing up his hair, pointed to a woman having done the deed. Women know that a different dress and hair-do can completely alter their own appearance. Miss Liang applied this method to a man—and that was a bad mistake.'

Judge Dee took a sip from the cup the sergeant had refilled for him, then resumed, 'As a matter of course it could also have been an elaborate scheme to inculpate Miss Liang. But I considered that a remote possibility. Miss Liang herself was our best chance. When the headman informed me that the dead beggar had been found at the back of her house, I knew that my theory must be correct. However, when we had gone inside I saw that she was a rather small and frail woman, who could never have bashed in the head of her tall victim. Therefore I at once looked around for some death-trap, and found it in the potted orchids on the high shelf, where the wilted plant supplied the final clue. She must have climbed up the ladder, probably asking Wang to steady it for her. Then she made some remark or other that made him turn his head, and smashed the pot down on his skull. These and other details we'll learn tomorrow when I question Miss Liang in the tribunal. Now as regards the role played by Mrs Kwang, I don't think she did more than help Miss Liang to concoct the scheme of getting the fictitious redemption fee out of Lo. Our charming hostess draws the line at murder; hers is a high-class establishment, remember!'

Sergeant Hoong nodded. 'Your Honour has not only uncovered a cruel murder, but at the same time saved Magistrate Lo from an alliance with a determined and evil woman!'

Judge Dee smiled faintly. 'Next time I meet Lo,' he said, 'I'll tell him about this case—without mentioning, of course, that I know it was he who patronized Miss Liang. My gay friend must have been visiting my district incognito! This case will teach him a lesson—I hope!'

Hoong discreetly refrained from commenting further on one of his master's colleagues. He remarked with a satisfied smile: 'So now all the points of this curious case have been cleared up!'

Judge Dee took a long draught from his tea. As he set the cup down he shook his head and said unhappily: 'No, Hoong. Not all the points.'

He thought he might as well tell the sergeant now about the ghostly apparition of the dead beggar, without which this murder would have been dismissed as an ordinary accident. But just as he was about to speak, his eldest son came rushing inside. Seeing his father's angry look, the boy said with a quick bow: 'Mother said we might take that nice lantern to our bedroom, sir!'

As his father nodded, the small fellow pushed an armchair up to one of the pillars. He climbed on the high backrest, reached up and unhooked the large lantern of painted silk hanging down from the eaves. He jumped down, lit the candle inside with his tinderbox, and held up the lantern for his father to see.

'It took Big Sister and me two days to make this, sir!' he said proudly. 'Therefore we didn't want Ah-kuei to spoil it. We like the Immortal Lee, he is such a pathetic, ugly old fellow!'

Pointing at the figure the children had painted on the lantern, the judge asked: 'Do you know his story?' When the boy shook his head, his father continued: 'Many, many years ago Lee was a very handsome young alchemist who had read all books and mastered all magic arts. He could detach his soul from his body and then float at will in the clouds, leaving his empty body behind, to resume it when he came down to earth again. One day, however, when Lee had carelessly left his body lying in a field, some farmers came upon it. They thought it was an abandoned corpse, and burned it. So when Lee came down, he found his own beautiful body gone. In despair he had to enter the corpse of a poor old crippled beggar which happened to be lying by the roadside, and Lee had to keep that ugly shape for ever. Although later he found the Elixir of Life, he could never undo that one mistake, and it was in that form that he entered the ranks of the Eight Immortals: Lee with the Crutch, the Immortal Beggar.'

The boy put the lantern down. 'I don't like him anymore!' he said with disdain. 'I'll tell Big Sister that Lee was a fool who only got what he deserved!'

He knelt down, wished his father and Hoong good night, and scurried away.

Judge Dee looked after him with an indulgent smile. He took up the lantern to blow out the candle inside. But suddenly he checked himself. He stared at the tall figure of the Immortal Beggar projected on the plaster wall. Then he tentatively turned the lantern round, as it would turn in the draught. He saw the ghostly shadow of the crippled old man move slowly along the wall, then disappear into the garden.

With a deep sigh the judge blew the candle out and put the lantern back on the floor. He said gravely to Sergeant Hoong, 'You were right after all, Hoong! All our doubts are solved— at least those about the mortal beggar. He was a fool. As to the Immortal Beggar—I am not too sure.' He rose and added with a wan smile, 'If we measure our knowledge not by what we know but by what we don't, we are just ignorant fools, Hoong, all of us! Let's go now and join my ladies.'

THE WRONG SWORD

This case also occurred in Poo-yang. As readers of The Chinese Bell Murders will remember, Poo-yang was bordered on one side by the Chin-hwa district, where Magistrate Lo held sway, and on the other by the district of Woo-yee, administered by the austere Magistrate Pan. The murder described in the present story happened in Judge Dee's absence; he had gone to Woo-yee to discuss with his colleague Pan a case involving both districts. The judge had set out from Poo-yang three days previously, taking with him Sergeant Hoong and Tao Gan, and leaving Ma Joong and Chiao Tai in charge of the tribunal. The three days had passed uneventfully for his two lieutenants; it was only on the last day, on the very evening that Judge Dee was expected back, that things suddenly began to happen.

'You pay for the fourth dozen stuffed crabs!' Ma Joong told Chiao Tai with satisfaction as he put the dice back into the box.

'They were worth it,' said Chiao Tai, smacking his lips. He took his wine beaker and emptied it in one draught.

Judge Dee's two burly lieutenants were sitting at a small table near the window, on the second floor of the Kingfisher Restaurant, one of their favourite haunts. Situated on the water-way that crosses the city of Poo-yang from north to south, its second-floor window offered a splendid view of the evening sun, setting beyond the western city wall.

The sounds of boisterous applause came up from the street below. Ma Joong poked his head out of the window and looked down at the crowd that had assembled on the river bank.

'It's that troupe of travelling actors which came here four days ago,' he remarked. 'In the afternoon they perform acrobatics in the street, at night they stage historical plays.'

'I know,' Chiao Tai said. 'The rice-dealer Lau helped them rent the yard of the old Taoist temple for setting up their stage. Lau came to the tribunal the other day for the permit. The leader of the troupe was with him—decent-looking fellow, Bao his name is. The troupe consists of his wife, his daughter and his son.' He refilled his beaker and added: 'I had thought of strolling over to the temple; I like a good play with lots of sword-fencing. But since our judge is away and we're responsible for everything, I don't like to leave the tribunal for long.'

'Well, here we have a grandstand seat for their acrobatic turns at least,' Ma Joong said contentedly. He turned his chair round to the window and put his folded arms on the sill. Chiao Tai followed his example.

In the street below a square reed mat had been spread out, surrounded by a dense crowd of spectators. A small boy of about eight was turning somersaults there with surprising agility. Two other actors, a tall lean man and a sturdy woman stood on the left and right of the mat with folded arms, and a young girl was squatting by the side of a bamboo box, evidently containing their paraphernalia. On top of the box was a low wooden rack; two long, shining swords were laid across it, one above the other. All four actors wore black jackets and wide trousers; red sashes were wound tightly round their waists, and red scarves round their heads. An old man dressed in a shabby blue gown was sitting on a tabouret close by, lustily beating the drum he held between his bony knees.

'Wish I could see that girl's face,' Ma Joong said wistfully. 'Look, Lau is there too; he seems to be in trouble!'

He pointed down at a neatly dressed, middle-aged man wearing a black gauze cap, who was standing behind the bamboo box. He was quarrelling with a huge ruffian whose unruly hair was bound up with a blue rag. He grabbed Lau's sleeve but Lau pushed him away. The two men paid no attention to the boy who was now walking around the reed mat on his hands, balancing a wine jar on the soles of his feet.

'I have never seen that tall rogue before,' Chiao Tai remarked. 'Must be from outside the city.'

'Now we'll get a good view of the wenches!' Ma Joong said with a grin.

The boy had finished. The leader of the troupe stood in the centre of the mat, legs apart and knees slightly bent. The sturdy

116

woman placed her right foot on his knee, then with one lithe movement climbed up onto his shoulders. At a shout from the man, the girl climbed up too, put one foot on the man's left shoulder, grabbed the woman's arm with one hand, and stretched out her other arm and leg. At almost the same time the boy followed her example and balanced himself on the man's right shoulder. As the human pyramid stood there precariously, the greybeard in the faded gown beat a frantic roll on his drum. The crowd burst out in loud shouts of approval.

The faces of the boy, the woman and the girl were only ten feet or so from Ma Joong and Chiao Tai. The latter whispered with enthusiasm: 'Look at the woman's splendid figure! Nice friendly face too!'

'I prefer the girl!' Ma Joong said eagerly.

'Much too young! The woman is about thirty, just right. Knows what's what!'

The drummer stopped; the woman and her two children jumped down from Bao's shoulders. All four actors made a graceful bow, then the girl went round among the spectators collecting coppers in a wooden bowl. Ma Joong pulled a string of cash from his sleeve and threw it down at her. She caught it expertly and rewarded him with a smile.

'That's literally throwing money away!' Chiao Tai remarked dryly.

'Call it an investment in a promising project!' Ma Joong countered with a smug grin. 'What's next?'

The boy was standing in the centre of the reed mat. He put his hands behind his back and lifted his chin. As the greybeard started to beat his drum, Bao bared his right arm, grabbed the sword lying on top of the rack, and with a movement quick as lightning plunged it deep into the boy's breast. Blood spurted out; the boy staggered backwards as his father pulled the sword out again. There were horrified cries from the crowd.

'I have seen that trick before,' Ma Joong said. 'Heaven knows how they do it! The sword looks genuine enough.' He turned away from the window and took his wine beaker.

The agonized cry of a woman rose above the confused murmur of voices. Chiao Tai, who had been looking down intently, suddenly jumped up. He snapped: 'That was no trick, brother! It was plain murder! Come along!'

The two men rushed down the stairs and ran outside. They elbowed their way through the excited crowd to the edge of the reed mat. The boy was lying on his back, his breast a mass of blood. His mother was kneeling by his side, sobbing convulsively as she stroked the small, still face. Bao and his daughter were standing there stock still, staring down with pale faces at the pitiful dead body. Bao still held the bloodstained sword.

Ma Joong wrenched it from his hand and asked angrily: 'Why did you do that?'

The actor woke from his stupor. Giving Ma Joong a dazed look, he stammered: 'It was the wrong sword!'

'I can explain, Mr Ma!' the rice-dealer Lau spoke up. 'It was an accident!'

A squat man came forward; it was the warden of the west quarter. Chiao Tai ordered him to roll the dead body in the reed mat and have it brought to the tribunal for examination by the coroner. As the warden gently made the mother rise, Chiao Tai said to Ma Joong, 'Let's take these people up to the dining-room, and try to get this straight!'

Ma Joong nodded. Taking the sword under his arm, he said to the rice-dealer, 'You come too, Mr Lau. And let the greybeard bring the box and that other sword along.'

He looked for the tall ruffian who had accosted Lau, but the fellow was nowhere to be seen.

Up on the second floor of the Kingfisher Restaurant Ma Joong told Bao, the two crying women and the old drummer to sit down at a corner table. He poured them wine from the jar he and Chiao Tai had been drinking from. He hoped that the strong liquor would help them get over the shock. Then he turned to the rice-dealer and ordered him to explain. He knew that the theatre was Lau's hobby, that he attended all shows given by travelling actors. His regular face with the short black moustache and goatee was pale and drawn. He adjusted his black gauze cap, then began diffidently:

'As you may know, Mr Ma, this man Bao is the leader of the

troupe, a fine actor and acrobat.' He paused, passed his hand over his face, then took the second sword which the old drummer had laid on the table. 'You may have seen these trick-swords,' he continued. 'The blade is hollow, and filled with pig's blood. It has a false point a couple of inches long, which slides back into the blade if the sword is pushed against something. Thus it appears as if the point penetrates deeply, the illusion being completed by the pig's blood spurting out. When the sword is pulled out, the point resumes its original position, being pushed out again by a rattan spiral hidden inside. You can see it for yourself!'

Ma Joong took the sword from him. He noticed a thin groove round it, a few inches below the blunt point. He turned round and pressed it against the wooden floor. The point slid into the blade, red blood spurted out. Mrs Bao started to scream. Her husband quickly put his arm round her shoulders. The girl remained sitting, still as a stone figure. The greybeard muttered angrily, pulling at his ragged beard.

'That wasn't too clever, brother!' Chiao Tai snapped.

'Had to verify it, didn't I?' Ma Joong said contritely. He took the real sword in his other hand, and balanced the two weapons carefully. 'These two swords are about the same weight,' he muttered. 'And they look exactly alike. Dangerous!'

'The trick-sword ought to have been lying on top of the rack,' Lau said, 'and the real sword below it. After the stabbing trick the boy would get up, and his father would perform a dance with the real sword.'

Bao had risen. Stepping up to Ma Joong, he asked hoarsely: 'Who exchanged the swords?' As Ma Joong only pursed his lips, Bao grabbed his shoulder and shouted: 'Who did it, I ask you?'

Ma Joong gently loosened his grip and made him sit down again. 'That's what we are going to find out,' he said. 'Are you quite sure that you put the trick-sword on top?'

'Of course! Haven't we been through that routine a hundred, a thousand times?'

Ma Joong shouted downstairs for more wine. He motioned Chiao Tai and Lau to follow him to the table in front of the window. When they had sat down he whispered to Lau, 'My mate

119

and I were looking out from this window here. We saw you and a tall ruffian standing close by the bamboo box and the sword rack. Who else was standing near you two?'

'I really couldn't say,' Lau replied with a frown. 'When the boy was doing his somersaults that tall rogue, who had been standing by my side for some time, suddenly asked me for money. When I refused he began to threaten me. I told him to make himself scarce. Then . . . it happened.'

'Who is he?' Chiao Tai asked.

'Never saw him before. Perhaps Bao knows.'

Chiao Tai got up and asked the actors. Bao, his wife and his daughter all shook their heads, but the old drummer said in a wheezing voice, 'I know him all right, sir! He came to our show in the temple yard every night, paid one copper only! He is a vagabond; his name is Hoo Ta-ma.'

'Did you see anyone else come near the sword rack?' Chiao Tai asked.

'How could I, seeing I had to keep my eyes on the performance all the time?' the greybeard replied indignantly. 'I only noticed Mr Lau and Hoo Ta-ma, because I happen to know both of them. But there were lots of others, all packed close. How could I see what was going on there?'

'I suppose you couldn't,' Chiao Tai said resignedly. 'And we couldn't have arrested the whole crowd.' Turning to Bao again, he asked: 'Did you notice anyone you know standing close to the mat?'

'I don't know anyone here,' Bao replied in a toneless voice. 'We have been to Woo-yee and Chin-hwa, but this is our first visit to this city. I only know Mr Lau. He introduced himself to me when I was surveying the temple yard for the setting up of our stage, and he kindly offered his help.'

Chiao Tai nodded. He liked Bao's open, intelligent face. He turned back to the others and said to Lau, 'You'd better take the actors back to their quarters, Mr Lau. Tell them that the magistrate is expected back here later tonight, and he'll investigate this foul murder at once. Tomorrow they'll have to attend the session of the tribunal, for the formalities. Then the boy's body will be handed back to them for burial.'

'Can I come too, Mr Chiao? Bao is a nice fellow; I'd like to do all I can to help him in this awful predicament.'

'You'll have to be there anyway!' Ma Joong said dryly. 'You are an important witness.'

He and Chiao Tai rose and said a few comforting words to the stricken family. When Lau had taken them and the greybeard downstairs, the two friends sat down again at the window table. Silently they emptied their wine beakers. While Ma Joong was refilling them he said, 'Well, I hope that's everything. Tonight we'll put it all before the judge. It'll be a hard nut to crack, I'd say. Even for him!'

He gave his friend a thoughtful look, but Chiao Tai made no comment. He idly watched the waiter who had come upstairs with a large oil lamp. When the waiter had gone, Chiao Tai banged his beaker down and said bitterly, 'What a dirty murder! Tricking a father into killing his own son, and before his mother's eyes! You know what? We've got to get the mean bastard who did it! Here and now!'

'I agree,' Ma Joong said slowly, 'but a murder is no small matter. I am not so sure that our judge would like us meddling in the investigation. One wrong move might spoil everything, you know!'

'If we do only what the judge would have ordered anyway, I don't see that we can do much harm.'

Ma Joong nodded. Then he said briskly: 'All right, I am with you! Here's luck!' Having emptied his cup, he added with a wry smile, 'This is a chance to prove our mettle! When those worthy citizens talk to us here, butter wouldn't melt in their mouths. But behind our backs they say we are just a couple of vulgar bullies, all brawn and no brain!'

'Up to a point,' Chiao Tai said judiciously, 'they are right. We are not men of letters, after all. That's why I wouldn't dream of tackling a case involving the gentry, for instance. But this murder is just the thing for us, for all concerned are the kind of people we are familiar with.'

'Let's plan out the investigation, then!' Ma Joong growled. He refilled their beakers.

'Our judge always starts by talking about motive and opportunity,' Chiao Tai began. 'In this case, the motive is as plain as a pikestaff. Since nobody could have had anything against that poor boy, the murderer must have hated Bao. Like poison.'

'Right. And since Bao is here in Poo-yang for the first time, our suspects are narrowed down to the people who have been in close contact with him and his troupe these last few days.'

'There still is the possibility that Bao met an old enemy here,' Chiao Tai objected.

'In that case Bao would have told us about him at once,' Ma Joong said. He thought hard for a while. 'I am not too sure that nobody could have had anything against the boy, you know. Youngsters like that have a knack of turning up in the most un-expected places; he could have seen or heard something he shouldn't have. Someone wanted to close the boy's mouth, and the sword-trick was a godsend.'

'Yes,' Chiao Tai admitted. 'Heavens, there are too many possi-bilities!' He sipped his wine, then frowned and put his beaker down. 'This stuff tastes funny!' he remarked astonished.

'It's the same we had before, but it doesn't taste right to me either! Tell you what, brother! Wine is only good when you are happy and carefree! You can't do real drinking with problems weighing on your mind!'

'That's why our judge is always sipping tea then, the poor sap!' Chiao Tai scowled at the wine jar, then grabbed it and put it down on the floor, under the table. Folding his muscular arms in his sleeves, he resumed: 'As to opportunity, both Lau and Hoo were standing close to the rack, so either of them could have exchanged the swords. What about their motives?'

Ma Joong rubbed his chin. After a while he answered, 'As regards Hoo, I can think of only one. Or two, rather. Meaning Mrs Bao and her daughter. Heavens, I wouldn't mind having a go at those wenches myself! Think of the acrobatic tricks they can do! Suppose Hoo wanted either of them or both, and Bao said hands-off, and Hoo took this badly?'

'Possible. If Hoo is a degenerate, mean type of scoundrel, he might take revenge on Bao in a dirty way like this. But what about Lau?'

'Out of the question! Lau is the old-fashioned, prim type. If he engaged in extramural amorous games, he'd sneak off to some discreet brothel. He wouldn't dare start something with an actress.'

'I agree that Hoo is our best chance,' Chiao Tai said. 'I'll go along now and have a talk with him. Then I'll look up Lau too, just for the sake of completeness, so to speak. You had better go to the temple, brother, and get to know more about the general background. Our judge will want to know everything about the Bao family, I expect.'

'All right, I'll pump the two women; that's the smoothest approach, I'd say!' He got up briskly.

'Maybe not as smooth as you think,' Chiao Tai said dryly as he rose also. 'Those two women are acrobats, remember! They know how to use their hands if you annoy them! Well, we'll meet later, in the tribunal.'

Chiao Tai went straight to the small winehouse in the east city where Sheng Pa, the head of the Beggars' Guild, had his headquarters.

The only occupant of the dingy taproom was a man of colossal proportions reclining in an armchair, snoring loudly. His mast-like arms were folded over his large bare belly, which protruded from under his worn-out black jacket.

Chiao Tai shook him roughly. The man woke up with a start. Giving Chiao Tai a baleful look, he said crossly, 'You would give a peaceful old man a fright! But sit down, anyway. Let me profit by your conversation.'

'I am in a hurry. You know a rogue called Hoo Ta-ma?'

Sheng Pa slowly shook his large head. 'No,' he said ponderously, 'I don't know him.'

Chiao Tai caught the crafty look that flashed through the other's eyes. He said impatiently, 'You may not have met him, but you must know about him, you fat crook! He's been seen in the yard of the old Taoist temple.'

'Don't call me names!' Sheng Pa said with a pained look. Then he added wistfully, 'Ah, that temple yard! My old headquarters! Those were the days, brother! Gay and carefree! Look at me

123

now, master of the guild, burdened with administrative duties!
I . . .'

'The only burden you carry is your belly,' Chiao Tai interrupted. 'Speak up! Where do I find Hoo?'

'Well,' Sheng Pa replied resignedly, 'if you must push matters to extremes . . . I have heard it said that a man who calls himself by that name can usually be found in a wine stall below the east city wall—the fifth one north from the East Gate, as a matter of fact. It's only hearsay, mind you, I . . .'

'Thank you kindly!' Chiao Tai rushed out.

In the street he stuffed his cap into his sleeve, and rumpled his hair. A brief walk brought him to a shed of old boards put up against the base of the city wall. He surveyed the dark, deserted neighbourhood, then pulled aside the door curtain and stepped inside.

The shed was dimly lit by a smoking oil lamp, and was filled with a nauseating stench of rancid oil and cheap liquor. An old man with bleary eyes was serving wine dregs behind a rickety bamboo counter. Three men in tattered gowns were standing about in front of it, Hoo Ta-ma's tall frame towering above the others.

Chiao Tai stood himself next to Hoo. The men eyed him indifferently; evidently they didn't know him for an officer of the tribunal. He ordered a drink. After he had taken a sip from the cracked rice-bowl that served as a wine cup, he spat on the floor and growled at Hoo: 'Filthy stuff! It's bad when you are down to your last coppers!'

A wry smile lit up Hoo's broad, sun-tanned face. Chiao Tai thought he looked like a rough-and-ready rascal, but not entirely unprepossessing. He resumed, 'You wouldn't know a job with something in it, would you?'

'No, I don't. Besides, I am the last man to ask, brother! I am having a spell of dirty luck, these days. Week ago I was supposed to pinch two cartloads of rice on the road, in Woo-yee. Easy job, only had to knock out the two carters. Affair had been nicely planned—on a lonely stretch, in the forest. My bad luck spoiled it.'

'You are getting too old, maybe!' Chiao Tai sneered.

'Shut up and listen! Just as I knock the first carter down, a small brat comes running round the corner. He looks me up and down and asks, silly-like: "What are you doing that for?" I hear noises, and jump into the undergrowth. From my hideout I see a tilt cart with travelling actors come round the corner. The second carter tells them the sad story, adding that I took to my heels. They move on together, rice-carts and all!'

'Bad luck!' Chiao Tai agreed. 'And you may be in for more of it too. Yesterday I saw a troupe performing in the street here, there was a boy doing somersaults. If that's the same brat, you'd better be careful. He might spot you.'

'Spotted me already! Caught me in the act again! With his sister, this second time! Can you imagine worse luck? But the brat had bad luck too. He's dead!'

Chiao Tai tightened his belt. This was a simple case, after all. He said affably, 'You certainly have bad luck, Hoo! I am an officer of the tribunal, and you are coming along with me!'

Hoo cursed obscenely, then barked at the two others, 'You heard him, the dirty running-dog of the tribunal! Let's beat the thief-catcher to pulp!'

The two vagabonds slowly shook their heads. The elder said, 'You don't belong here, brother. Settle your accounts yourself!'

'Rot in hell!' And to Chiao Tai: 'Come outside, I'll get you or you'll get me!'

A beggar who was loitering in the dark alley scurried away when he saw the two men come out and take up boxers' stances.

Hoo started with a quick blow at Chiao Tai's jaw, but he parried it expertly and followed up with an elbow thrust in Hoo's face. The other ducked and grabbed Chiao Tai's waist with his long, muscular arms. Chiao Tai realized that in a body-to-body fight Hoo was no mean opponent; he was of the same height, but much heavier, and he tried to throw Chiao Tai by utilizing this advantage. Soon both men were panting heavily. But Chiao Tai knew more about technique, and he succeeded in slipping out of the other's bear-like hug. He stepped back, then placed an accurate blow in Hoo's face that closed his left eye. Hoo shook his head, then came again for him, growling angrily.

Chiao Tai was on his guard for foul tricks, but apparently Hoo didn't go in for them. He made a feint, then gave Chiao Tai a blow in his midriff that would have floored him if he hadn't ducked and caught it on his breastbone. Chiao Tai feigned to be winded and staggered back. Hoo aimed a straight blow at his jaw to finish him off. Chiao Tai caught Hoo's fist in both hands, ducked under his arm and threw him over his back. There was a snapping sound as the rogue's shoulder dislocated and he crashed to the ground, hitting his head on a stone with a sickening thud. He lay quite still.

Chiao Tai went into the shed again and told the greybeard to give him a rope, then to run out and call the warden and his men.

Chiao Tai tied Hoo's legs securely together. Then he squatted down and waited for the warden. Hoo was carried to the tribunal on an improvised stretcher. Chiao Tai ordered the jail keeper to put Hoo in a cell, call the coroner and have him revive the unconscious man, then set his shoulder.

These things having been attended to, Chiao Tai walked over to the chancery deep in thought. There was one point that was worrying him. Perhaps the case was not so simple after all.

In the meantime Ma Joong had walked from the Kingfisher Restaurant back to the tribunal, where he had taken a bath. When he had put on a nice clean robe he strolled to the Taoist temple.

A mixed crowd was standing about below the raised stage of bamboo poles, lighted by two large paper lanterns. The show had started already, for Bao couldn't afford to let the death of his son interfere with the theatrical routine. He, his wife and his daughter, all three dressed in gorgeous stage costumes, stood in front of two superimposed tables representing a throne. Mrs Bao sang to the accompaniment of a strident fiddle.

Ma Joong went to the bamboo cage next to the stage where the greybeard was vigorously scraping his two-stringed violin, at the same time working a brass gong with his right foot. Ma Joong waited till he put the violin aside and changed to a pair of wooden clappers. He nudged him and asked with a meaningful grin:

'Where can I meet the women?'

The old man pointed with his bearded chin at the stepladder behind him, then beat his clappers extra hard.

Ma Joong climbed up to the improvised green-room, separated from the stage by screens of bamboo matting. There was only a cheap dressing-table littered with platters for rouge and powder, and one low tabouret.

Loud shouts of approval from the audience indicated that the actors had reached the end of a scene. The dirty blue curtain was drawn aside and Miss Bao came in.

She was dressed for the part of a princess, in a long green robe glittering with brass-foil ornaments, and wearing an elaborate headdress decorated with garish paper flowers. Two long tresses of glossy black hair hung down from her temples. Although her face was covered with the thick layer of stage make-up, Ma Joong thought that she still looked remarkably attractive. She gave him a quick look, then sat down on the tabouret. Leaning towards the mirror to inspect her painted eyebrows, she asked listlessly:

'Is there any news?'

'Nothing in particular!' Ma Joong replied cheerfully. 'I just came round for a talk with a charming girl!'

She turned her head and gave him a contemptuous look. 'If you think that'll get you anywhere with me,' she snapped, 'you are wrong!'

'I wanted to talk about your parents!' he said, taken aback by this abrupt rebuff.

'Parents? About my mother, you mean! Well, for her you need no intermediary, she's always open to a fair business proposition!'

Suddenly she buried her face in her hands and started to sob. He stepped up to her and patted her on the back. 'Now don't get upset, dear! Of course this terrible affair of your brother has . . .'

'He wasn't my brother!' she interrupted him. 'This life . . . I can't stand it any longer! My mother a whore, my father a stupid fool who dotes on her . . . You know what part I am acting now? I am the daughter of a noble king and his chaste queen! How's that for a joke?' She angrily shook her head, then started to dab her face energetically with a wad of paper. She resumed in a calmer voice, 'Imagine, mother produced that boy half a year ago, out of nothing! Told father she had made a little mistake, eight years ago. The fellow who had got her into trouble had looked after the boy all that time, then decided he couldn't keep him any longer. Father gave in, as always . . .' She bit her lips.

'Have you any idea,' Ma Joong asked, 'who could have played that infernal trick on your father tonight? Has he met an old enemy here, perhaps?'

'Why should those swords have been exchanged intentionally?' she said curtly. 'My father could have made a mistake, couldn't he? The two swords look exactly the same, you know. They have to, else the trick wouldn't look genuine.'

'Your father seemed sure someone had changed them,' Ma Joong remarked.

Suddenly she stamped her foot on the floor and exclaimed: 'What a life! I hate it! Heaven be praised that I'll be making a new start soon. At last I have met a decent fellow who is willing to pay father a handsome dowry, and take me as a concubine.'

'Life as a concubine isn't always so great, you know!'

'I won't be a concubine for long, my friend! His wife is ailing and the doctors don't give her more than a year or so.'

'Who's the lucky fellow, anyway?'

She hesitated a moment before she replied, 'I'll tell you because you are an officer of the tribunal. Keep it quiet for a while, will you? It's the rice-dealer, Lau. He has had bad luck in business lately, and he doesn't want to speak to my father before he can put the money on the table. Lau is a bit older than me, of course, and he's got old-fashioned ideas in his head, but I tell you I am sick and tired of those so-called gay young blades, who just want to sleep with you once, and then on to the next!'

'How did you come to know Lau?'

'Met him the very day we came here to Poo-yang. He offered father help in renting this yard. Lau took a liking to me at once, he . . .'

Her voice was drowned in the deafening applause from outside. She jumped up, put her headdress straight and said hurriedly:

'I must go on now! Good-bye!'

She disappeared through the curtain.

Ma Joong found his friend sitting all alone in the deserted

128

'I AM THE DAUGHTER OF A NOBLE KING AND HIS CHASTE
QUEEN! HOW'S THAT FOR A JOKE?'

chancery. Chiao Tai looked up and said, 'Seems our case is solved, brother! I have a suspect under lock and key here in jail!'

'Good!' Ma Joong pulled up a chair and listened to Chiao Tai's story. Then he told him about his interview with Miss Bao. 'Combining our information,' he concluded, 'it appears that Miss Bao had a fling with Hoo, in between her meetings with the devoted Lau. Just to keep in good form, I suppose. Well, what are you looking so worried for?'

'I forgot to tell you just now,' Chiao Tai replied slowly, 'that Hoo Ta-ma didn't want to come nice and quiet like, I had to go through some fisticuffs with him. The fellow fought cleanly, not one dirty kick or blow. I can imagine Hoo breaking that boy's neck in a fit of rage when he caught him peeping while he was busy with his sister; but to play that mean trick of exchanging the swords . . . No, brother, that isn't in character, I tell you!'

'Some people have all kinds of characters, all at the same time,' Ma Joong said with a shrug. 'Let's go and see how the bastard is getting along.'

They got up and walked to the jail behind the courtroom. Chiao Tai told the keeper to fetch the senior scribe, to act as witness and makes notes of the interrogation.

Hoo was sitting on the couch in his small dark cell, his hands and feet chained to the wall. When Chiao Tai lifted the candle, Hoo looked up at him and said sourly:

'I hate to admit it, dogshead, but that was a nifty throw!'

'Thank you for nothing! Tell me more about this robbery you bungled.'

'Don't see why I shouldn't! Assault and battery, that's all you have on me. Only knocked out one carter, didn't even touch the rice bales.'

'How had you planned to get rid of those two cartloads?' Ma Joong asked curiously. 'You can't sell so much rice without roping in the guild merchants.'

'Sell nothing!' Hoo said with a grin. 'I'd have heaved the bales into the river, the whole lot!' Seeing their astonished expressions he added: 'That rice had gone bad, all of it, you see. Fellow who had sold it wanted it stolen, then the guild would have had to make good. Since I bungled the job, the rice was duly delivered, found bad, and the dealer had to pay back all the money he had received from the buyer. Bad luck all around. However, I still thought the fellow owed me a silver piece for my trouble. But when I spoke to him about it, he refused to cough up!'

'Who is he?' Chiao Tai asked.

'One of your local rice-dealers, fellow called Lau.'

Chiao Tai shot Ma Joong a perplexed look. The latter asked: 'How did you come to know Lau? You are from Woo-yee, aren't you?'

'Old friend of mine! I've known him for years; he regularly visits Woo-yee. He is a smooth customer, Lau is, always ready for a bit of swindling. Sanctimonious rascal had a love-nest in Woo-yee; the woman he kept there was a friend of a wench I used to go around with—that's how I was introduced to Lau. Some people have funny tastes, though. Mine was a strapping wench, but Lau's an elderly hag. Yet he had a boy by her, my girl told me. Perhaps the hag looked good eight years ago. Heaven knows!'

'Talking about wenches,' Ma Joong said, 'how did you get on to Miss Bao?'

'Simple! Happened to see her on the stage the first night they played here, and took a liking to her. Tried that night, and the next, to get better acquainted, but nothing doing! Yesterday night I tried again—had nothing better to do while waiting for Lau to come across with the silver. It was late at night, after the performance, she looked tired; her nerves were all on edge. But when I asked her anyway, she replied, "All right. But you'd better be good, for it's my last fling!" Well, we slipped into an empty street stall in a quiet corner of the yard there, but just after we got started, that boy popped up, looking for his sister. I told him to make himself scarce, which he did. Whether it was that interruption or lack of proper training I don't know, but anyway I was disappointed by what followed. That's how it goes, you know; sometimes it turns out much better than you expected, other times it's worse. But what I got I got gratis, so who am I to complain?'

'I saw you quarrel with Lau in the street,' Chiao Tai said. 'You two were standing close by that sword rack. Did you see anybody fiddle with those swords?'

Hoo wrinkled his corrugated forehead. Then he shook his head and answered, 'I had to divide my attention between that bastard Lau and the two women all the time, you see. The daughter was standing right in front of me before the boy started on his somersaults—I could have pinched her behind. Seeing that she is so standoffish, I pinched her mother's instead when she came to shift the bamboo box a bit to the side. Only reward I got was a dirty look, though. Meanwhile Lau had tried to slip away from me; he nearly stumbled over the box when I dragged him back by the sleeve. Anybody could have switched those two toothpicks on the rack.'

'Including you !' Ma Joong said coldly.

Hoo tried to jump up, the rattling chains tautened. He sank back with a cry of pain. 'So that's what you are after, you bastards !' he shouted. 'Hang that foul murder on me, eh? Of all the mean tricks . . .' He looked at Chiao Tai and burst out, 'You can't do that to me, officer ! I swear that I never killed a man. I've knocked some fellows about a bit, but that's all. To kill a youngster in such a . . .'

'Better think it over !' Ma Joong said gruffly. 'We have ways and means to get the truth out of you !'

'Go to hell !' Hoo shouted.

Back in the chancery Ma Joong and Chiao Tai sat down at the large desk against the back wall. The scribe seated himself opposite them, close by the candle. The two friends watched him morosely while he took from the drawer a few sheets of blank paper and moistened his writing-brush to work out his notes of the interrogation. After a long pause Ma Joong said :

'Yes, I agree with you that Hoo probably didn't do it. The bastard did do one thing, though. He messed up the case for us— thoroughly !'

Chiao Tai nodded unhappily. 'Lau is a crook, and a lecher to boot, despite his prim air. First kept a woman in Woo-yee, now tries to get Miss Bao in his clutches. Our miss didn't live like a nun, but she's still a juicy bit. Lau had no earthly reason to kill the boy or to spite Bao, but we'll put him behind bars anyway. Our judge will want to check Hoo's statements with him.'

'Why not let the headman get the three Baos and the old musician here tonight as well? Then our judge will have all the human data before him, so to speak. Tomorrow morning, during the session of the court, he'll be able to get down to business right away and settle this case!'

'That's a good idea.'

When Ma Joong came back, the old scribe had finished his notes. After he had read them out aloud, and Ma Joong and Chiao Tai had approved them, the latter said, 'Since you wield that writing-brush so deftly, grandpa, you'd better take down our reports too!'

The scribe resignedly took a sheaf of new sheets. Ma Joong leaned back into his chair, pushed his cap away from his fore-head, and started upon his story, beginning with how they had witnessed the murder from the window of the Kingfisher Restaurant. Then Chiao Tai dictated his report on the arrest of Hoo Ta-ma. It was hard work, for they knew that Judge Dee disliked wordy statements, yet insisted on having all details in full. When they were ready at last their faces were wet with perspiration.

Thus Judge Dee found them when, an hour before midnight, he came in, clad in his brown travelling-robe. He looked tired and worried. As the three men jumped up quickly, the judge asked sharply:

'What is this all about? When I stepped down from my palankeen the headman told me that you had two men locked up in jail as murder suspects, and four witnesses summoned!'

'Well, sir,' Ma Joong began diffidently, 'it's rather a sordid murder, of a young boy. My mate and I did a little investigating; all we did is written down here. It began . . .'

'Come to my private office!' Judge Dee interrupted curtly. 'Bring the papers along!'

He ordered the scribe to bring a large pot of hot tea to his office, then went outside followed by his two lieutenants.

Sitting down in the large armchair behind his desk, Judge Dee said, 'That affair in Woo-yee was settled all right. My colleague Pan is an efficient fellow, nice to work with. Sergeant Hoong and Tao Gan are staying on there for another day, to look after a few details.' He took a sip of hot tea, then settled back into his chair with the sheaf of papers.

Ma Joong and Chiao Tai sat stiffly erect on the tabourets in front of the desk. Their throats were parched, but they didn't notice it. They anxiously watched Judge Dee's face for his reactions.

First the judge creased his bushy eyebrows in a deep frown. But as he read on his face gradually relaxed. When he had finished the last page, he reread some passages, and asked the two men to quote some of their conversations verbatim. Then he threw the papers on the desk. Sitting up, he said with a slow smile:

'Congratulations! Both of you have done very well. You not only carried out the routine work expected from you, but also proved that you are able to take independent action. The two arrests were amply justified.'

His two lieutenants grinned broadly. Ma Joong grabbed the teapot and quickly poured a cup for Chiao Tai and himself.

'Now then,' Judge Dee resumed, 'let's see where we are. In the first place, the facts now before us are insufficient to prove that it was murder. Bao was in a hurry, for after the acrobatics they had to rush back to the temple for the stage performance; besides, it was getting dark. Thus it is quite possible that Bao placed the wrong sword on top, by mistake. It's true that he himself suggested foul play, but perhaps he was afraid of being accused of criminal negligence, and those travelling actors stand in deadly fear of the authorities.' The judge paused and stroked his long beard. 'On the other hand, the facts you learned about the people connected with this occurrence suggest various reasons why some of them might have intentionally switched the swords. Including Bao.'

'Why should Bao want to kill the boy?' Ma Joong exclaimed.

'To take vengeance on his unfaithful wife and her paramour, the rice-dealer Lau.' Silencing his astonished lieutenants with his raised hand, Judge Dee continued: 'You don't doubt that the boy in Lau's love-nest in Woo-yee was Mrs Bao's illegitimate son, do you? Lau is interested in the stage; I suppose he met Mrs Bao when the troupe was performing in Woo-yee. When their son was born, they entrusted the child to an old crone who kept a house of assignation there. Eight years later Mrs Bao decided to take the child, which meant that she had to confess her infidelity to her husband. Miss Bao stated that her father took this very calmly, but Bao's indifference may have been feigned. Today, when Bao saw Lau standing near the sword rack, he realized that this was a splendid opportunity to take vengeance on his unfaithful wife, get rid of the illegitimate child and involve Lau in a murder case—all at the same time. For we can also formulate a strong case against Lau.'

Again Ma Joong and Chiao Tai wanted to speak, but again the judge silenced them and went on: 'Lau had the opportunity, the special knowledge of stage-props required for utilizing the opportunity, and one can imagine more than one motive. Blackmail is the first that comes to mind. When Bao's troupe comes to Pooyang, Lau offers his services, perhaps hoping to renew his affair with Mrs Bao. But Bao and his wife try to blackmail him—the boy is living proof of Lau's extra-marital activities in Woo-yee. By changing the swords, Lau would destroy that proof, and he could close Bao's mouth by threatening to accuse him of having killed, out of jealousy, his wife's illegitimate child.

'Then, we also have Mrs Bao. Her daughter gave Ma Joong to understand that her mother is practically a prostitute, and the emotions of such women are often difficult to gauge. When Mrs Bao realized that Lau, her former lover, was now transferring his affection to her daughter, she may well have taken revenge on him by having his son killed. However, we shouldn't attach too much importance to Miss Bao's statements, for she seems a rather unbalanced girl. She doesn't hesitate to call her mother a whore and her father a fool, but she herself makes no bones about sleeping with a vagabond on the eve of concluding a more permanent arrangement with Lau. We must find out, by the way, whether Miss Bao knew that Lau had been her mother's lover.' He paused, eyed his two lieutenants speculatively, 'I am only surveying all possibilities, mind you. It's no use going further into all this before we know more about the emotional relationships of the persons concerned.'

Judge Dee took the papers up again and leafed through them,

135

studying a passage here and there. Putting them down, he said pensively, 'We must remember that these travelling actors live in two quite different worlds. On the stage they have to identify themselves completely with the great men and women of our national past. Off-stage they are impoverished outcasts who can barely scrape enough together for their daily needs. Such a double life can distort a person's character.'

The judge fell silent. He took a sip from his tea, then sat for a while deep in thought, slowly caressing his sidewhiskers.

'Does Your Honour agree that Hoo is innocent?' Chiao Tai asked.

'No. At least not for the time being. It is true that Hoo Ta-ma made a favourable impression on you two, and for all I know your estimate of him may be entirely correct. However, those vagrant bullies have sometimes strange sides to their character. Hoo went out of his way to stress that it was Miss Bao's fault that their rendezvous was not a success, and he mentioned the interruption caused by the boy as a possible cause. But it may well have been the other way round, namely that it was Hoo himself who failed. He may have feared that his virility was permanently impaired, and such an obsession could inspire in him a violent hatred of that unfortunate boy. I thought it odd that Hoo spoke at such great length about his amorous exploits to two officers interrogating him in jail. It makes one suspect that he is obsessed by the problem to such a degree that he simply has to talk about it. And since Hoo had several talks with the old drummer, he also had a chance to learn about the trick-sword. On the other hand, however, Hoo's expanding on his love-life may just as well have been an innocent desire to show off.' Judge Dee rose and added briskly, 'I'll now have a look at the people concerned. This office is too small. Tell the headman to bring them all to the reception hall. And let the scribe call two clerks, so that the proceedings can be taken down properly. While you two are attending to this, I'll go and have a quick bath.'

The spacious reception hall was very bright. The wall-candles had all been lit, and on the desk in the centre stood two large candelabras of wrought silver. Bao, his wife and his daughter, and

136

the old musician, were seated on chairs in front of the desk. Hoo stood between two constables on the left; Lau on the opposite side, also flanked by two constables. The senior scribe and his two assistants sat at a smaller table. The actors and the prisoners studiously ignored each other; all were staring straight ahead. The hall was deadly quiet.

Suddenly the double-doors were pushed open by the headman of the constables. Judge Dee entered, followed by Ma Joong and Chiao Tai. The judge was clad in a plain, dark-grey robe, and wore a small black skull-cap on his head. All bowed deeply as he went to the desk and sat down in the large armchair of carved ebony. His two lieutenants stood on either side of him.

Judge Dee first surveyed the two prisoners, the sullen Hoo and the prim, rather fussy Lau. He thought that his two lieutenants had described these two men very accurately. Then he silently studied the three actors. Noticing how wan and tired they looked, he thought of the long and heavy day they had behind them, and he felt some compunction about playing on their emotions, as he intended to do. He sighed, then cleared his throat and spoke in an even tone:

'Before I question the two prisoners, I first want to establish the exact family-relationship that links those present here with the dead boy.' Looking fixedly at Mrs Bao, he went on: 'I am informed, Mrs Bao, that the boy was your illegitimate child. Is that correct?'

'Yes, Your Honour,' she replied in a voice that sounded very tired.

'Why didn't you take the child to you until it was eight years old?'

'Because I hesitated to tell my husband, and because the father had promised to take care of it. At one time I thought I loved the man, sir; because of him I left my husband for more than a year. The man had told me that his wife was mortally ill, and that after her death he would marry me. But after I had found out what a mean person he really was, I broke off relations. I didn't meet him again until, half a year ago, I ran into him when we were performing in the capital. He wanted to renew our relationship, and when I said no, he said in that case there was no

137

reason why he should pay any longer for the boy. Then I told my husband everything.' She gave the actor by her side an affectionate look and went on: 'Understanding man as he is, he didn't scold me. He said that the boy was just what he needed to complete our troupe, and that he would make a good acrobat out of him. And he did indeed! People look down on our profession, sir, but my husband and I take pride in it. My husband loved the boy as if he were his own son, he . . .'

She bit her twitching lips. After a brief pause Judge Dee asked: 'Did you tell your husband who your lover was?'

'No, Your Honour. The man treated me shabbily, but I saw no reason why I should ruin his reputation. Neither do I see a reason for doing so now. And my husband never asked me.'

'I see,' the judge said. The woman's frank statement bore the hallmark of truth. Now he knew who had murdered the boy. And also the motive: the boy had had to be silenced, as Ma Joong had correctly supposed at the very beginning. But thereafter his lieutenant had failed to apply this theory to the facts that had come to light. Tugging at his moustache, the judge reflected ruefully that although he now knew who had exchanged the swords, there wasn't a shred of evidence. If he didn't act quickly, he would never be able to prove who committed the crime. He must make the criminal confess here and now, before he had time to realize the full implications of Mrs Bao's statement. He curtly told the headman: 'Bring the accused Lau before me!'

When the rice-dealer was standing in front of the desk, Judge Dee addressed him harshly: 'Lau, here in Poo-yang you have carefully built up a reputation as an honest rice-dealer and a man of impeccable morals, but I know all about your activities in Woo-yee. You tried to deceive your own guild, and you kept a mistress there. Hoo Ta-ma supplied additional details. I advise you to answer my questions truthfully! Speak up, do you admit that it was you who had a liaison with Mrs Bao, eight years ago?'

'I do,' Lau replied in an unsteady voice. 'I beg Your Honour to . . .'

There was a strangled cry. Miss Bao had risen from her chair. Clenching her hands, she stared at Lau with wide, burning eyes. He stepped back, muttering something. Suddenly she screamed:

'You unspeakable cad! May heaven and hell curse me for foolishly believing your string of lies! Played the same trick on my mother, eh? And to think that because I was a credulous fool, was afraid, afraid that the brat would tell you about my meeting Hoo, I put the wrong sword on top! I'll kill you too, you . . .'

She went for the cowering man, raising her hands like claws. The two constables quickly stepped forward and grabbed her arms. On a sign from the judge they led her away, screaming and fighting like a wildcat.

Her parents looked after her with unbelieving eyes. Then her mother burst out in sobs.

Judge Dee rapped his knuckles on the table. 'Tomorrow I shall hear Miss Bao's full confession in court. As to you, Lau, I shall institute a thorough inquiry into all your affairs, and I shall see to it that you get a long prison term. I dislike people of your type, Lau. Hoo Ta-ma, you shall be sentenced to one year compulsory labour with the sappers of our Northern Army. That'll give you a chance to prove what you are worth; in due time you'll perhaps be enlisted as a regular soldier.' Turning to the headman, he added: 'Lead the two prisoners back to jail!'

For a while the judge looked silently at the actor and his wife. She had stopped crying; now she sat very still, her eyes downcast. Bao looked worriedly at her, the lines on his expressive actor's face had deepened. Judge Dee addressed them gently:

'Your daughter could not cope with the hard life fate had allotted to her, and it thoroughly corrupted her character. I must propose the death penalty for her. That means that you lose, on one and the same day, both your daughter and your son. But time shall heal this cruel wound. You two are still in the prime of life, you love each other and your profession, and that twofold devotion shall be a lasting support. Though everything will seem dark to you now, remember that even behind the darkest clouds of night there shines the moon of dawn.'

They rose, made a deep bow and took their leave.

THE COFFINS OF THE EMPEROR

The events described in this story took place when Judge Dee was occupying his fourth post as magistrate, namely of Lanfang, an isolated district on the western frontier of the mighty T'ang Empire. Here he met with considerable trouble when taking up his duties, as described in the novel The Chinese Maze Murders. *The present story tells about the grave crisis that threatened the Empire two years later, in the winter of the year* A.D. 672, *and how Judge Dee succeeded in solving, on one and the same night, two difficult problems, one affecting the fate of the nation, the other the fate of two humble people.*

As soon as Judge Dee had entered the dining-room on the restaurant's top floor, he knew that the banquet would be a dismal affair. The light of two large silver candelabras shone on the beautiful antique furniture, but the spacious room was heated by only one small brazier, where two or three pieces of coal were dying in the embers. The padded curtains of embroidered silk could not keep out the cold draught, reminding one of the snowy plains that stretched out for thousands of miles beyond the western frontier of the Chinese Empire.

At the round table sat only one man, the thin, elderly magistrate of Ta-shih-kou, this remote boundary district. The two girls who were standing behind his chair looked listlessly at the tall, bearded newcomer.

Magistrate Kwang rose hastily and came to meet Judge Dee.

'I profoundly apologize for these poor arrangements!' he said with a bleak smile. 'I had invited also two colonels and two guildmasters, but the colonels were suddenly summoned to the Marshal's headquarters, and the guildmasters were wanted by the Quartermaster-General. This emergency . . .' He raised his hands in a helpless gesture.

'The main thing is that I shall now profit from your instructive conversation!' Judge Dee said politely.

His host led him to the table and introduced the very young girl on his left as Tearose, and the other as Jasmine. Both were gaudily dressed and wore cheap finery—they were common prostitutes rather than the refined courtesans one would expect at a dinner party. But Judge Dee knew that all the courtesans of Ta-shih-kou were now reserved for the high-ranking officers of the Marshal's headquarters. When Jasmine had filled Judge Dee's wine beaker, Magistrate Kwang raised his own and said:

'I welcome you, Dee, as my esteemed colleague of the neighbour-district and my honoured guest. Let's drink to the victory of our Imperial Army!'

'To victory!' Judge Dee said and emptied his beaker in one draught.

From the street below came the rumble of iron-studded cart-wheels on the frozen ground.

'That'll be the troops going to the front at last for our counter-offensive,' the judge said with satisfaction.

Kwang listened intently. He sadly shook his head. 'No,' he said curtly, 'they are going too slowly. They are coming back from the battlefield.'

Judge Dee rose, pulled the curtain aside and opened the window, braving the icy wind. In the eerie moonlight he saw down below a long file of carts, drawn by emaciated horses. They were packed with wounded soldiers and long shapes covered with canvas. He quickly closed the window.

'Let's eat!' Kwang said, pointing with his chopsticks at the silver bowls and platters on the table. Each contained only a small quantity of salted vegetables, a few dried-out slices of ham and cooked beans.

'Coolie fare in silver vessels—that sums up the situation!' Kwang spoke bitterly. 'Before the war my district had plenty of everything. Now all food is getting scarce. If this doesn't change soon we'll have a famine on our hands.'

Judge Dee wanted to console him, but he quickly put his hand to his mouth. A racking cough shook his powerful frame. His colleague gave him a worried look and asked, 'Has the lung epidemic spread to your district too?'

The judge waited till the attack had passed, then he quickly emptied his beaker and replied hoarsely, 'Only a few isolated cases, and none really bad. In a milder form, like mine.'

'You are lucky,' Kwang said dryly. 'Here most of those who get it start spitting blood in a day or two. They are dying like rats. I hope your quarters are comfortable,' he added anxiously.

'Oh yes, I have a good room at one of the larger inns,' Judge Dee replied. In fact he had to share a draughty attic with three officers, but he didn't like to distress his host further. Kwang hadn't been able to accommodate him in his official residence because it had been requisitioned by the army, and the magistrate had been obliged to move with his entire family into a small ramshackle house. It was a strange situation; in normal times a magistrate was well-nigh all-powerful, the highest authority in his district. But now the army had taken over. 'I'll go back to Lan-fang tomorrow morning,' the judge resumed. 'There are many things to be attended to, for in my district also food is getting scarce.'

Kwang nodded gloomily. Then he asked: 'Why did the Marshal summon you? It's a good two days' journey from Lan-fang to here, and the roads are bad.'

'The Uigurs have their tents on the other side of the river that borders my district,' Judge Dee replied. 'The Marshal wanted to know whether they were likely to join the Tartar armies. I told him that . . .' He broke off and looked dubiously at the two girls. The Tartar spies were everywhere.

'They are all right,' Kwang said quickly.

'Well, I informed the Marshal that the Uigurs can only bring two thousand men in the field, and that their Khan went on a prolonged hunting trip to Central Asia, just before the Tartar emissaries arrived at his camp to ask him to join forces with them. The Uigur Khan is a wise man. We have his favourite son as hostage, you see, in the capital.'

'Two thousand men won't make any difference either way,' Kwang remarked. 'Those accursed Tartars have three hundred thousand men standing at our frontier, ready to strike. Our front is crumbling under their probing attacks, and the Marshal keeps his two hundred thousand men idle here, instead of starting the promised counteroffensive.'

142

For a while the two men ate in silence, while the girls kept their cups filled. When they had finished the beans and salted vegetables, Magistrate Kwang looked up and asked Tearose impatiently, 'Where is the rice?'

'The waiter said they don't have any, sir,' the girl replied.

'Nonsense!' the magistrate exclaimed angrily. He rose and said to Judge Dee: 'Excuse me a moment, will you? I'll see to this myself!'

When he had gone downstairs with Tearose, the other girl said softly to Judge Dee, 'Would you do me a great favour, sir?'

The judge looked up at her. She was a not unattractive woman of about twenty. But the thick layer of rouge on her face could not mask her sallow complexion and hollow cheeks. Her eyes were unnaturally wide and had a feverish glow.

'What is it?' he asked.

'I am feeling ill, sir. If you could leave early and take me with you, I would gladly receive you after I have rested awhile.'

He noticed that her legs were trembling with fatigue. 'I'll be glad to,' he replied. 'But after I've seen you home, I shall go on to my own lodging.' He added with a thin smile: 'I am not feeling too well myself, you know.'

She gave him a grateful look.

When Magistrate Kwang and Tearose came back, Kwang said contritely, 'I am very sorry, Dee, but it's true. There is no rice left.'

'Well,' Judge Dee said, 'I enjoyed our meeting very much. I also think that Jasmine here is quite attractive. Would you think it very rude if I asked to be excused now?'

Kwang protested that it was far too early to part, but it was clear that he too thought this the best solution. He conducted Judge Dee downstairs and took leave of him in the hall. Jasmine helped the judge don his heavy fur coat, then they went out into the cold street. Sedan-chairs were not to be had for love or money; all the bearers had been enlisted for the army transports.

The carts with the dead and wounded were still filing through the streets. Often the judge and his companion had to press themselves against the wall of a house to let dispatch-riders pass, driving their weary horses on with obscene curses.

Jasmine led the judge down a narrow side street to a small hovel, leaning against a high, dark godown. Two struggling pine trees flanked the cracked door, their branches bent low under the load of frozen snow.

Judge Dee took a silver piece from his sleeve. Handing it to her, he said, 'Well, I'll be going on now, my inn . . .' A violent attack of coughing seized him.

'You'll come inside and at least drink something hot,' she said firmly. 'You aren't fit to walk about as you are.' She opened the door and dragged the judge inside, still coughing.

The attack subsided only after she had taken his fur coat and made him sit down in the bamboo chair at the rickety tea-table. It was very warm in the small dark room; the copper brazier in the corner was heaped with glowing coals. Noticing his astonished glance, she said with a sneer; 'That's the advantage of being a prostitute nowadays. We get plenty of coal, army issue. Serve our gallant soldiers!'

She took the candle, lit it at the brazier, then put it back on the table. She disappeared through the door curtain in the back wall. Judge Dee surveyed the room in the flickering light of the candle. Against the wall opposite him stood a large bedstead; its curtains were drawn, revealing rumpled quilts and a soiled double-pillow.

Suddenly he heard a queer sound. He looked round. It came from behind a faded blue curtain, which was covering something close to the wall. It flashed through his mind that this could well be a trap. The military police flogged thieves on the street corners till their bones lay bare, yet robbery and assault were rampant in the city. He rose quickly, stepped up to the curtain and ripped it aside.

He blushed despite himself. A wooden crib stood against the wall. The small round head of a baby emerged from under a thick, patched quilt. It stared up at him with its large wise eyes. The judge hurriedly pulled the curtain close, and resumed his seat.

The woman came in carrying a large teapot. Pouring him a

cup, she said, 'Here, drink this. It's a special kind of tea; they say it cures a cough.'

She went behind the curtain and came back with the child in her arms. She carried it to the bed, pulled the quilts straight with one hand and turned the pillow over.

'Excuse this mess,' she said at she laid the child on the bed. 'I had a customer here just before the magistrate had me called to attend our dinner.' With the unconcern marking women of her profession, she took off her robe. Clad only in her wide trousers, she sat on the bed and leaned back against the pillow with a sigh of relief. Then she took up the child and laid it against her left breast. It started drinking contentedly.

Judge Dee sipped the medicinal tea; it had an agreeable bitter taste. After a while he asked her: 'How old is your child?'

'Two months,' the woman replied listlessly. 'It's a boy.'

His eye fell on the long white scars on her shoulders; one broad weal sorely mutilated her right breast. She looked up and saw his glance. She said indifferently, 'Oh, they didn't mean to do that, it was my own fault. When they were flogging me, I tried to wrench myself loose, and one tongue of the scourge curled over my shoulder and tore my breast.'

'Why were you flogged?' the judge asked.

'Too long a story to tell!' she said curtly. She concentrated her attention on the child.

Judge Dee finished his tea in silence. His breathing came easier now, but his head was still throbbing with a dull ache. When he had drunk a second cup, Jasmine carried the baby back to the crib and pulled the curtain shut. She came to the table, stretched herself and yawned. Pointing at the bedstead, she asked, 'What about it? I have rested a bit now, and the tea hardly covers what you paid me.'

'Your tea is excellent,' the judge said wearily; 'it more than covers what I gave you.' In order not to offend her he added quickly, 'I wouldn't risk infecting you with this accursed lung trouble. I'll have one more cup, then I'll be on my way.'

'As you like!' Sitting down opposite him, she added, 'I'll have a cup myself, my throat is parched.'

In the street footsteps crunched in the frozen snow. It was the men of the night watch. They beat midnight on their wooden clappers. Jasmine shrank in her seat. Putting her hand to her throat, she gasped, 'Midnight already?'

'Yes,' Judge Dee said worriedly, 'if we don't start our counter-offensive very soon, I fear the Tartar hordes will break through and overrun this area. We'll drive them back again, of course, but since you have that nice child, wouldn't it be wiser if you packed up and went east tomorrow morning?'

She was looking straight ahead, agony in her feverish eyes. Then she spoke, half to herself, 'Six hours to go!' Looking at the judge, she added: 'My child? At dawn his father will be beheaded.'

Judge Dee set his cup down. 'Beheaded?' he exclaimed. 'I am sorry. Who is he?'

'A captain, name of Woo.'

'What did he do?'

'Nothing.'

'You aren't beheaded for nothing!' the judge remarked crossly.

'He was falsely accused. They said he strangled the wife of a fellow officer. He was court-martialled and condemned to death. He has been in the military jail now for about a year, waiting for the confirmation. It came today.'

Judge Dee tugged at his moustache. 'I have often worked together with the military police,' he said. 'Their judicial system is cruder than our civilian procedure, but I have always found them efficient, and very conscientious. They don't make many mistakes.'

'They did in this case,' Jasmine said. She added resignedly: 'Nothing can be done; it's too late.'

'Yes, since he is to be executed at dawn, there isn't much we can do about it,' the judge agreed. He thought for a while, then resumed, 'But why not tell me about it? You would get my mind off my own worries and perhaps it might help you to pass the time.'

'Well,' she said with a shrug, 'I am feeling too miserable to sleep anyway. Here it is. About a year and a half ago, two captains of the garrison here in Ta-shih-kou used to frequent the

146

licensed quarters. One was called Pan, the other Woo. They had
to work together because they belonged to the same branch of
the service, but they didn't get along at all; they were as different as can be. Pan was a milksop with a smooth face, a dandy
who looked more like a student than an officer. With all his fine
talk he was a nasty piece, and the girls didn't like him. Woo was
just the opposite, a rough-and-ready boy, a good boxer and swords-
man, quick with his hands and quick with a joke. They used to
say that the soldiers would go through fire and water for him.
He wasn't what you'd call handsome, but I loved him. And he
would have no one but me. He paid the owner of the brothel I
belong to at regular times so that I didn't have to sleep with
the first comer. He promised to buy and marry me as soon as he
got his promotion, that's why I didn't mind having his child.
Usually we get rid of them when we are pregnant or sell them.
But I wanted mine.' She emptied her cup, pushed a lock away
from her forehead, and went on, 'So far so good. Then, one night
about ten months ago, Pan came home and found his wife lying
there strangled to death, and Woo standing by her bed, looking
dazed. Pan called in a passing patrol of the military police, and
accused Woo of having murdered his wife. Both were brought
before the military tribunal. Pan said that Woo kept bothering
his wife, who wouldn't have him. The slimy bastard said he
warned Woo many times to leave her alone; he hadn't wanted to
report him to the colonel because Woo was his fellow-officer!
Well, Pan added that Woo knew that Pan was on night duty
in the armoury that evening, so he had gone to Pan's house and
again tried to bed with his wife. She had refused, and Woo had
flown into a rage and strangled her. That was all.'

'What did Woo have to say to that?' Judge Dee asked.

'Woo said that Pan was a dirty liar. That he knew that Pan
hated him, and that Pan himself had strangled his wife in order
to ruin him.'

'Not a very clever fellow, that captain of yours,' the judge remarked dryly.

'Listen, will you? Woo said that when he passed by the armoury
that night, Pan hailed him and asked him to go round to his
house and see whether his wife needed anything, for she had felt

indisposed that afternoon. When Woo got there, the front door was open, the servants gone. No one answered his calls, so he went into the bedroom where he found her dead body. Then Pan came rushing inside and started hollering for the military police.'

'A queer story,' Judge Dee said. 'How did the military judge formulate his verdict? But no, you wouldn't know that, of course.'

'I do. I was there myself, sneaked in with the others. Wet all over with fright, I tell you, for if they catch a whore in a military establishment she gets scourged. Well, the colonel said that Woo was guilty of adultery with the wife of a fellow-officer, and sentenced him to have his head chopped off. He said he wouldn't say too much about murder, for his men had found out that Pan himself had sent his servants away after dinner that night, and as soon as he had gone on duty at the armoury, he had told the military police that he had been warned about thieves in his neighbourhood, and asked them to keep an eye on his house. The colonel said that it was possible Pan had discovered that his wife was carrying on with Woo, and that he had therefore strangled her. That was his right; according to the law, he could have killed Woo too, if he had caught them in the act, as they call it. But maybe Pan had been afraid to tackle Woo, and had chosen this roundabout way of getting at him. Anyway that was neither here nor there, the colonel said. The fact was that Woo had played games with the wife of a fellow-officer, and that was bad for the morale of the army. Therefore he had to be beheaded.'

She fell silent. Judge Dee caressed his sidewhiskers. After a while he said, 'On the face of it I would say that the colonel was perfectly right. His verdict agrees with the brief character sketch you gave me of the two men concerned. Why are you so sure that Woo didn't have an affair with Pan's wife?'

'Because Woo loved me, and wouldn't even look at another woman,' she replied promptly.

Judge Dee thought that this was a typical woman's argument. To change the subject, he asked: 'Who flogged you, and why?

'It's all such a stupid story!' she said in a forlorn voice. 'After the session I was furious with Woo. I had discovered that I was pregnant, and the mean skunk had been carrying on with the

Pan woman all the time, behind my back! So I rushed to the jail and got inside by telling the guards I was Woo's sister. When I saw him I spat in his face, called him a treacherous lecher, and ran off again. But when I was so far gone I couldn't work any more, I got to thinking things over, and I knew I had been a silly fool, and that Woo loved me. So eight weeks ago, after our child had been born and I was a little better, I again went to the military prison to tell Woo I was sorry. But Woo must have told the guards how I fooled them the time before—and he was right, too, the way I had shouted at him! As soon as I was inside they lashed me to the rack and gave me a flogging. I was in luck, I knew the soldier who handled the scourge; he didn't hit too hard, else the army would have had to supply a coffin then and there. As it was, my back and shoulders were cut to ribbons and I was bleeding like a pig, but I am no weakling and I made it. As strong as a farmhand, father used to say of me before he had to sell me to pay the rent for our field. Then there came rumours about the Tartars planning an attack. The garrison commander was called to the capital, and the war started. What with one thing and another Woo's case dragged on. This morning the decision came, and at dawn they'll chop his head off.'

Suddenly she buried her face in her hands and started to sob. The judge slowly stroked his long black beard, waiting till she had calmed down. Then he asked:

'Was the Pans' marriage a happy one?'

'How do I know? Think I slept under their bed?'

'Did they have children?'

'No.'

'How long had they been married?'

'Let me see. About a year and a half—I know that. When I first met the two captains, Woo told me that Pan had just been called home by his father to marry the woman his parents had got for him.'

'Do you happen to know his father's name?'

'No. Pan only used to brag that his father was a big noise in Soochow.'

'That must be Pan Wei-liang, the Prefect,' Judge Dee said at once. 'He is a famous man, a great student of ancient history. I

149

have never met him, but I have read many of his books. Quite good. Is his son still here?'

'Yes, attached to headquarters. If you admire those Pans so much, you'd better go there and make friends with the mean bastard!' she added contemptuously.

Judge Dee rose. 'I'll do that,' he said, half to himself.

She mouthed an obscene word. 'You are all the same, all of you!' she snapped. 'Am I glad I am just an honest whore! The gentleman is choosy, doesn't want to sleep with a woman with half a breast gone, eh? Want your money back?'

'Keep it!' Judge Dee said calmly.

'Go to hell!' she said. She spat on the floor and turned her back on him.

Judge Dee silently put on his fur coat and left.

While he was walking through the main street, still crowded with soldiers, he reflected that things didn't look too good. Even if he found Captain Pan, and even if he succeeded in extracting from him the fact he needed for the testing of his theory, he would then have to try to obtain an audience with the Marshal, for only he could, at this stage, order a stay of execution. And the Marshal was fully occupied by weighty issues, the fate of the Empire was in the balance. Moreover, that fierce soldier was not notorious for his gentle manner. Judge Dee set his teeth. If the Empire had come to such a pass that a judge couldn't prevent an innocent man from being beheaded . . .

The Marshal's headquarters were located in the so-called Hunting Palace, an immense compound that the present Emperor had built for his beloved eldest son, who had died young. The Crown Prince had been fond of hunting on the western frontier. He had died on a hunting expedition there, and it had been his wish to be buried in Ta-shih-kou. His sarcophagus had been placed in a vault there, and later that of his Princess beside it.

Judge Dee had some trouble in getting admitted by the guards, who looked with suspicion on every civilian. But at last he was led to a small, draughty waiting-room, and an orderly took his red visiting-card to Captain Pan. After a long wait a young officer came in. The tight-fitting mail jacket and the broad swordbelt accentuated his slender figure, and the iron helmet set off his handsome but cold face, smooth but for a small black moustache. He saluted stiffly, then stood waiting in haughty silence till the judge addressed him. A district magistrate ranked much higher, of course, than an army captain, but Pan's attitude suggested that in wartime things were different.

'Sit down, sit down!' Judge Dee said jovially. 'A promise is a promise, I always say! And better late than never!'

Captain Pan sat down on the other side of the tea-table, looking politely astonished.

'Half a year ago,' the judge continued, 'while passing through Soochow on my way to Lan-fang, I had a long conversation with your father. I also am a student of history, you know, in my spare time! When I was taking my leave, he said: "My eldest son is serving in Ta-shih-kou, your neighbour-district. If you should happen to pass by there, do me a favour and have a look how he's doing. The boy had awfully bad luck." Well, yesterday the Marshal summoned me, and before returning to Lan-fang I wanted to keep my promise.'

'That's most kind of you, sir!' Pan muttered, confused. 'Please excuse my rudeness just now. I didn't know . . . and I am in a terrible state. The bad situation at the front, you see . . .' He shouted an order. A soldier brought a pot of tea. 'Did . . . did my father tell you about the tragedy, sir?'

'Only that your young wife was murdered here last year. Accept my sincere . . .'

'He shouldn't have forced me to marry, sir!' the captain burst out. 'I told him . . . tried to tell him . . . but he was always too busy, never had time . . .' With an effort Pan took a hold of himself, and continued, 'I thought I was too young to marry, you see. Wanted my father to postpone it. For a few years, till I would've been stationed in a large city, for instance. Give me time to . . . to sort things out.'

'Were you in love with another girl?'

'Heaven forbid!' the young officer exclaimed. 'No sir, it was simply that I felt I was not the marrying kind. Not yet.'

'Was she murdered by robbers?'

Captain Pan sombrely shook his head. His face had gone

151

a deadly pale. 'The murderer was a fellow-officer of mine, sir. One of those disgusting woman-chasers; you could never have a decent, clean conversation with him. Always talking about women, women, always letting himself be caught in their filthy little games . . .' The young man spat out those last words. He quickly gulped down the tea, then added in a dull voice, 'He tried to seduce my wife, and strangled her when she refused. He'll be beheaded at dawn.' Suddenly he buried his face in his hands.

Judge Dee silently observed the stricken youngster for a while. Then he said softly: 'Yes, you had very bad luck indeed.' He rose and resumed in a businesslike manner, 'I must see the Marshal again. Please take me there.'

Captain Pan got up quickly. As he conducted the judge down a long corridor where orderlies were rushing to and fro, he said: 'I can take you only as far as the anteroom, sir. Only members of the High Command are allowed beyond.'

'That'll do,' Judge Dee said.

Captain Pan showed the judge into a hall, crowded with officers, then said he would wait outside to lead the judge back to the main gate. As soon as the judge had entered, the hubbub of voices ceased abruptly. A colonel stepped up to him. After a cursory glance at Judge Dee's cap he asked coldly: 'What can I do for you, Magistrate?'

'I have to see the Marshal on urgent business.'

'Impossible!' the colonel said abruptly. 'The Marshal is in conference. I have strict orders to admit nobody.'

'A human life is at stake,' the judge said gravely.

'A human life, you say!' the colonel exclaimed with a sneer. 'The Marshal is deliberating on two hundred thousand human lives that are at stake, Magistrate! May I lead the way?'

Judge Dee grew pale. He had failed. Piloting the judge politely but firmly to the exit, the colonel said: 'I trust that you'll understand, Magistrate. . . .'

'Magistrate!' shouted another colonel who came rushing inside. Despite the cold his face was covered with sweat. 'Do you happen to know where a colleague of yours is, called Dee?'

'I am Magistrate Dee,' the judge replied.

'Heaven be praised! I have been looking for you for hours! The Marshal wants you!'

He dragged the judge by his sleeve through a door at the back of the anteroom into a semi-dark passage. Thick felt hangings dampened all sound. He opened the heavy door at the end, and let the judge go inside.

It was curiously still in the enormous palace hall. A group of high-ranking officers in resplendent armour stood round a monumental desk, piled with maps and papers. All were looking silently at the giant who was pacing the floor in front of it, his hands clasped behind his back.

He wore an ordinary mail jacket with battered, iron shoulder-plates and the baggy leather trousers of a cavalry man. But on top of his high helmet the golden marshal's dragon raised its horned head. As the Marshal walked to and fro with heavy tread, he let the point of the broad sword that was dangling from his belt clatter carelessly on the delicately carved, marble floor-tiles.

Judge Dee knelt down. The colonel approached the Marshal. Standing stiffly at attention, he said something in a clipped voice. 'Dee?' the Marshal barked. 'Don't need the fellow anymore, send him away! No, wait! I still have a couple of hours before I order the retreat.' Then he shouted at the judge: 'Hey there, stop crawling on the floor! Come here!'

Judge Dee rose hurriedly, went up to the Marshal and made a deep bow. Then he righted himself. The judge was a tall man, but the Marshal topped him by at least two inches. Hooking his thumbs in his swordbelt, the giant glared at the judge with his fierce right eye. His left eye was covered by a black band—it had been pierced by a barbarian arrow during the northern campaign.

'You are good at riddles, they say, eh, Dee? Well, I'll show you a riddle!' Turning to the desk, he shouted: 'Lew! Mao!'

Two men wearing generals' armour hurriedly detached themselves from the group round the table. Judge Dee recognized the lean general in the shining golden armour as Lew, commander of the left wing. The broad-shouldered, squat man wearing a golden cuirass and a silver helmet was Mao, commanding general of the military police. Only Sang, the commander of the right wing, was missing. With the Marshal these three were the highest military leaders; in this national crisis the Emperor had placed the fate of the Chinese people and the dynasty in their hands. The judge made a low bow. The two generals gave him a stony look.

The Marshal strode through the hall and kicked a door open. They silently passed through a number of broad, empty corridors, the iron boots of the three officers resounding hollowly on the marble floor. Then they descended a broad staircase. At the bottom two palace guards sprang to attention. At a sign of the Marshal they slowly pushed open a heavy double-gate.

They entered a colossal vault, dimly lit by tall silver oil lamps, placed at regular intervals in recesses in the high, windowless walls. In the centre of the vault stood two enormous coffins, lacquered a bright red, the colour of resurrection. They were of identical size, each measuring about ten by thirty foot, and over fifteen foot high.

The Marshal bowed, and the three others followed his example. Then the Marshal turned to Judge Dee and said, pointing at the coffins, 'Here is your riddle, Dee! This afternoon, just when I was about to order the offensive, General Sang came and accused Lew here of high treason. Said that Lew had contacted the Tartar Khan and agreed that as soon as we would attack, Lew would join the Tartar dogs with his troops. Later Lew would get the southern half of the Empire as a reward. The proof? Sang said that Lew had concealed in the coffin of the Crown Prince two hundred suits of armour complete with helmets and swords, and marked with the special sign of the traitors. At the right moment Lew's confederates in the High Command would break the coffin open, don those marked suits of armour and massacre all the staff officers here who aren't in the plot.'

Judge Dee started and looked quickly at General Lew. The lean man stood there stiffly erect, staring ahead with a white, taut face.

'I trust Lew as I trust myself,' the Marshal went on, aggressively thrusting his bearded chin forward, 'but Sang has a long and honourable career behind him, and I can't take any chances. I must verify the accusation, and quick. The plans for our counter-offensive are ready. Lew will head a vanguard of fifteen thousand

'YOU ARE GOOD AT RIDDLES, THEY SAY, EH, DEE?' THE
MARSHAL GROWLED

men and drive a wedge into the Tartar hordes. Then I'll follow up with a hundred and fifty thousand men and drive the dogs back into their own steppes. But there are signs that the wind is going to shift; if I wait too long we'll have to fight with snow and hail blowing right into our faces.

'I have examined the coffin of the Crown Prince for hours, together with Mao's best men, but we can find no sign that it has been tampered with. Sang maintains they excised a large section of the lacquer coating, made a hole, pushed the stuff inside and replaced the section of coating. According to him, there are experts who can do this without leaving a trace. Maybe there are, but I must have positive proof. But I can't desecrate the coffin of the Emperor's beloved son by breaking it open—I may not even scratch it without the special permission of His Majesty—and it'll take at least six days before I can get word from the capital. On the other hand I can't open the offensive before I have made sure that Sang's accusation is false. If I can't do that in two hours, I shall have to order a general retreat. Set to work, Dee!'

The judge walked around the coffin of the Crown Prince, then he also examined cursorily that of the Princess. Pointing at a few long poles that were lying on the floor, he asked, 'What are these for?'

'I had the coffin tilted,' General Mao said coldly, 'in order to verify whether the bottom hadn't been tampered with. All that was humanly possible has been done.'

Judge Dee nodded. He said pensively, 'I once read a description of this palace. I remember that it said that the August Body was first placed in a box of solid gold, which was then placed in one of silver, and that in turn in a case of lead. The empty space around it was filled up with the articles of adornment and court costumes of the Crown Prince. The sarcophagus itself consists of thick logs of cedarwood, covered on the outside with a coat of lacquer. The same procedure was followed two years later, when the Princess died. Since the Princess had been fond of boating, behind the palace a large artificial lake was made, with models of the boats used by the Princess and her court ladies. Is that correct?'

156

'Of course,' the Marshal growled. 'It's common knowledge. Don't stand there talking twaddle, Dee! Come to the point!'

'Could you get me a hundred sappers, sir?'

'What for? Didn't I tell you we can't tamper with that coffin?'

'I fear the Tartars also know all about these coffins, sir. Should they temporarily occupy the city, they'll break the coffins open to loot them. In order to prevent the coffins from being desecrated by the barbarians, I propose to sink them to the bottom of the lake.'

The Marshal looked at him dumbfounded. Then he roared: 'You accursed fool! Don't you know the coffins are hollow? They'll never sink. You . . .'

'They aren't meant to, sir!' Judge Dee said quickly. 'But the plan to sink them provides us with a valid reason for deplacing them.'

The Marshal glared at him with his one fierce eye. Suddenly he shouted: 'By heaven, I think you've got it, Dee!' Turning to General Mao, he barked: 'Get me a hundred sappers here, with cables and rollers! At once!'

After Mao had rushed to the staircase, the Marshal started pacing the floor, muttering to himself. General Lew covertly observed the judge. Judge Dee remained standing there in front of the coffin of the Crown Prince, staring at it silently, his arms folded in his long sleeves.

Soon General Mao came back. Scores of small, squat men swarmed inside behind him. They wore jackets and trousers of brown leather and peaked caps of the same material, with long neck- and ear-flaps. Some carried long round poles, others rolls of thick cable. It was the sappers corps, expert at digging tunnels, rigging machines for scaling city walls, blocking rivers and harbours with underwater barriers, and all the other special skills used in warfare.

When the Marshal had given their commander his instructions, a dozen sappers rushed to the high gate at the back of the vault, and opened it. The bleak moonlight shone on a broad marble terrace. Three stairs descended into the water of the lake beyond, which was covered by a thin layer of ice.

The other sappers crowded round and over the coffin of the

157

Crown Prince like so many busy ants. One heard hardly a sound, for the sappers transmit orders by finger-talk only. They are so quiet they can dig a tunnel right under a building, the occupants becoming aware of what is happening only when the walls and the floor suddenly cave in. Thirty sappers tilted the coffin of the Crown Prince, using long poles as levers; one team placed rollers under it, another slung thick cables round the huge sarcophagus.

The Marshal watched them for a while, then he went outside and on to the terrace, followed by Dee and the generals. Silently they remained standing at the water's edge, looking out over the frozen lake.

Suddenly they heard a low rumbling sound behind them. Slowly the enormous coffin came rolling out of the gate. Dozens of sappers pulled it along by thick cables, while others kept placing new rollers underneath it. The coffin was drawn across the terrace, then let down into the water as if it was the hulk of a ship being launched. The ice cracked, the coffin rocked up and down for a while, then settled with about two-thirds of it under water. A cold wind blew over the frozen lake, and Judge Dee started to cough violently. He pulled his neckcloth up over the lower part of his face, beckoned the commander of the sappers and pointed at the coffin of the Princess in the vault behind them.

Again there was a rumbling sound. The second coffin came rolling across the terrace. The sappers let it down into the water where it remained floating next to that of the Crown Prince. The Marshal stooped and peered at the two coffins, comparing the waterlines. There was hardly any difference, if anything the coffin of the Princess was slightly heavier than that of the Crown Prince.

The Marshal righted himself. He hit General Lew a resounding clap on his shoulder. 'I knew I could trust you, Lew!' he shouted. 'What are you waiting for, man? Give the signal, go ahead with your troops! I'll follow in six hours. Good luck!'

A slow smile lit up the general's stern features. He saluted, then turned round and strode off. The commander of the sappers came and said respectfully to the Marshal: 'We shall now weigh the coffins with heavy chains and rocks, sir, then we . . .'

'I have made a mistake,' the Marshal interrupted him curtly.

158

'Have them drawn on land again, and replace them in their original position.' He barked at General Mao: 'Go with a hundred men to Sang's camp outside the West Gate. Arrest him on the charge of high treason, and convey him in chains to the capital. General Kao shall take over his troops.' Then he turned to Judge Dee, who was still coughing. 'You get it, don't you? Sang is older than Lew, he couldn't swallow Lew's appointment to the same rank. It was Sang, that son of a dog, who conspired with the Khan, don't you see? His fantastic accusation was meant only to stop our counteroffensive. He would have attacked us together with the Tartars as soon as we started the retreat. Stop that blasted coughing, Dee! It annoys me. We are through here, come along!'

The council room was now seething with activity. Large maps had been spread out on the floor. The staff officers were checking all details of the planned counteroffensive. A general said excitedly to the Marshal: 'What about adding five thousand men to the force behind these hills here, sir?'

The Marshal stooped over the map. Soon they were deep in a complicated technical discussion. Judge Dee looked anxiously at the large water-clock in the corner. The floater indicated that it would be dawn in one hour. He stepped up to the Marshal and asked diffidently: 'May I take the liberty of asking you a favour, sir?'

The Marshal righted himself. He asked peevishly: 'Eh? What is it now?'

'I would like you to review a case against a captain, sir. He's going to be beheaded at dawn, but he is innocent.'

The Marshal grew purple in his face. He roared: 'With the fate of our Empire in the balance, you dare to bother me, the Marshal, with the life of one wretched man?'

Judge Dee looked steadily into the one rolling eye. He said quietly: 'A thousand men must be sacrificed if military necessity dictates it, sir. But not even one man must be lost if it's not strictly necessary.'

The Marshal burst out in obscene curses, but he suddenly checked himself. With a wry smile he said: 'If ever you get sick

159

of that tawdry civilian paperwork, Dee, you come and see me. By God, I'll make a general officer out of you! Review the case, you say? Nonsense, I'll settle it, here and now! Give your orders!'

Judge Dee turned to the colonel who had rushed towards them when he heard the Marshal cursing. The judge said, 'At the door of the anteroom a captain called Pan is waiting for me. He falsely accused another captain of murder. Could you bring him here?'

'Bring also his immediate superior!' the Marshal added. 'At once!'

As the colonel hastened to the door, a low, wailing blast came from outside. It swelled in volume, penetrating the thick walls of the palace. It was the long brass trumpets, blowing the signal to assemble for the attack.

The Marshal squared his wide shoulders. He said with a broad smile: 'Listen, Dee! That's the finest music that ever was!' Then he turned again to the maps on the floor.

Judge Dee looked fixedly at the entrance. The colonel was back in a remarkably short time. An elderly officer and Captain Pan followed him. The judge said to the Marshal, 'They are here, sir.'

The Marshal swung round, put his thumbs in his swordbelt and scowled at the two men. They stood stiffly at attention, with rapt eyes. It was the first time they had ever seen the greatest soldier of the Empire face to face. The giant growled at the elderly officer: 'Report on this captain!'

'Excellent administrator, good disciplinarian. Can't get along with the men, no battle experience . . .' The officer rattled it off.

'Your case?' the Marshal asked Judge Dee.

The judge addressed the young captain coldly: 'Captain Pan, you weren't fit to marry. You don't like women. You liked your colleague Captain Woo, but he spurned you. Then you strangled your wife, and falsely accused Woo of the crime.'

'Is that true?' the Marshal barked at Pan.

'Yes, sir!' the captain replied as if in a trance.

'Take him outside,' the Marshal ordered the colonel, 'and have him flogged to death slowly, with the thin rattan.'

'I plead clemency, sir!' Judge Dee interposed quickly. 'This

160

captain had to marry at his father's command. Nature directed him differently, and he couldn't cope with the resulting problems. I propose the simple death penalty.'

'Granted!' And to Pan: 'Can you die as an officer?'

'Yes, sir!' Pan said again.

'Assist the captain!' the Marshal rasped at the elder officer.

Captain Pan loosened his purple neckcloth and handed it to his immediate superior. Then he drew his sword. Kneeling in front of the Marshal, Pan took the hilt of the sword in his right hand, and grabbed the point with his left. The sharp edge cut deeply into his fingers, but he didn't seem to notice it. The elder officer stepped up close to the kneeling man, holding the neckcloth spread out in his hands. Raising his head, Pan looked up at the towering figure of the Marshal. He called out:

'Long live the Emperor!'

Then, with one savage gesture, he cut his throat. The elder officer quickly tied the neckcloth tightly round the neck of the sagging man, staunching the blood. The Marshal nodded. He said to Pan's superior, 'Captain Pan died as an officer. See to it that he is buried as one!' And to the judge: 'You look after that other fellow. Freed, reinstated to his former rank, and so on.' Then he bent over the map again and barked at the general: 'Put an extra five thousand at the entrance of this valley here!'

As the four orderlies carried the dead body of Pan outside, Judge Dee went to the large desk, grabbed a writing-brush and quickly jotted down a few lines on a sheet of official paper of the High Command. A colonel impressed on it the large square seal of the Marshal, then countersigned it. Before running outside Judge Dee cast a quick look at the water-clock. He still had half an hour.

It took him a long time to cover the short distance between the Palace and the Military Jail. The streets were crowded with mounted soldiers; they rode in rows six abreast, holding high their long halberds, so greatly feared by the Tartars. Their horses were well fed and their armour shone in the red rays of dawn. It was General Lew's vanguard, the pick of the Imperial army. Then there came the deep sound of rolling drums, calling up the Marshal's own men to join their colours. The great counteroffensive had begun.

The paper with the Marshal's seal caused Judge Dee to be admitted at once to the prison commandant. A sturdily built youngster was brought in by four guards; his thick wrestler's neck had been bared already for the sword of the executioner. The commandant read out the document to him, then he ordered an adjutant to assist Captain Woo in donning his armour. When Woo had put on his helmet, the commandant himself handed him back his sword. Judge Dee saw that although Woo didn't look too clever, he had a pleasant, open face. 'Come along!' he said to him.

Captain Woo stared dumbfounded at his black judge's cap, then asked: 'How did you get involved in this case, Magistrate?'

'Oh,' Judge Dee replied vaguely, 'I happened to be at Headquarters when your case was reviewed. Since they are all very busy there now, they told me to take care of the formalities.'

When they stepped out into the street Captain Woo muttered: 'I was in this accursed jain almost a year. I have no place to go.'

'You can come along with me,' Judge Dee said.

As they were walking along the captain listened to the rolling of the drums. 'So we are attacking at last, eh?' he said morosely. 'Well, I am just in time to join my company. At least I'll die an honourable death.'

'Why should you deliberately seek death?' the judge asked.

'Why? Because I am a stupid fool, that's why! I never touched that Mrs Pan, but I betrayed a fine woman who came to see me in jail. The military police flogged her to death.'

Judge Dee remained silent. Now they were passing through a quiet back street. He halted in front of a small hovel, built against an empty godown.

'Where are we?' Captain Woo asked, astonished.

'A plucky woman, and the son she bore you are living here,' the judge answered curtly. 'This is your home, Captain. Good-bye.'

He quickly walked on.

As Judge Dee rounded the street corner, a cold blast blew full into his face. He pulled his neckcloth up over his nose and mouth, stifling a cough. He hoped that the servants would be on hand already in his inn. He longed for a large cup of hot tea.

MURDER ON NEW YEAR'S EVE

The scene of this story is also laid in Lan-fang. As a rule a magistrate's term of office was three years. But at the end of the year A.D. 674, when Judge Dee had been serving four years in Lan-fang, there was still no news from the capital. This is the story of what happened on the last evening of that dreary year. In the criminal cases previously solved by Judge Dee his theories always proved right in the end. However, the reader will see that in this particular case Judge Dee made two big mistakes. But, contrary to the rule, this time two wrongs made a right!

When Judge Dee had put away the last file and locked the drawer of his desk he suddenly shivered. He rose and, pulling his padded house-robe closer round his tall frame, he walked across his cold, empty private office to the window. He pushed it open, but after a brief glance at the dark courtyard of the tribunal outside, he quickly pulled it shut. The snow had stopped but a gust of icy wind had nearly blown out the candle on his desk.

The judge went to the couch against the back wall. With a sigh he started to fold back the quilts. That night, the last of the weary year that had passed, the fourth of his stay in Lan-fang, he would sleep in his office. For his own house at the back of the tribunal compound was deserted except for a few servants. Two months before, his First Lady had set out to visit her aged mother in her home town, and his two other wives and his children had accompanied her, together with his faithful old adviser Sergeant Hoong. They would be back early in spring—but spring seemed very far away on this cold and dreary night.

Judge Dee took up the teapot to pour himself a last cup of tea. He found to his dismay that it had grown cold. He was about to clap his hands to summon a clerk, then remembered that he had given the personnel of the tribunal the night off, including his three personal assistants. The only men about would be the constables on guard duty at the main gate.

Pulling his house-bonnet over his ears, he took up the candle and walked through the dark, deserted chancery to the guard-house.

The four constables squatting round the blazing log fire in the centre of the stone floor jumped up when they saw Judge Dee enter and hastily set their helmets straight. The judge could see only the broad back of their headman. He was leaning out of the window cursing violently at someone outside.

'Hey there!' Judge Dee barked at him. When the headman turned round and bowed deeply, he said curtly, 'Better mind your language on the last day of the year!'

The headman muttered something about an insolent ragamuffin who dared to bother the tribunal so late at night. 'The small monkey wants me to find his mother for him!' he added disgustedly. 'Do they take me for a nursemaid?'

'Hardly that!' Judge Dee said dryly. 'But what is it all about?' He stepped up to the window and looked out.

In the street below the tiny boy was cowering against the wall for shelter against the icy wind. The moonlight shone on his tear-stained face. He cried: 'It is all . . . all over the floor! I slipped and fell in it . . . And Mother is gone!'

He stared at his small hands, then tried to rub them clean on his thin, patched jacket. Judge Dee saw the red smears. Quickly turning round, he ordered the headman, 'Get my horse and follow me with two men!'

As soon as he was outside, the judge lifted the boy up and placed him on his saddle. Then he put his foot in the stirrup and slowly mounted behind him. Wincing, he remembered how not so long ago he could still jump on his horse. But a touch of rheumatism had been bothering him of late. He suddenly felt tired, and old. Four years in Lan-fang . . . With an effort he took hold of himself. He said in a cheerful voice to the sobbing boy, 'Now we'll go together and find your mother for you! Who is your father, and where do you live?'

'My father is pedlar Wang,' said the boy, swallowing his tears. 'We live in the second alley to the west of the Temple of Confucius, not far from the watergate.'

'That's easy!' Judge Dee said. He carefully guided his horse along the snow-covered street. The headman and two constables rode silently behind him. A strong gust of wind blew the snow from the roofs, the fine particles striking their faces like so many needles. Wiping his eyes, the judge asked again, 'What is your name, small boy?'

'I am called Hsiao-pao, sir,' he answered in a trembling voice.

'Hsiao-pao, that means Small Treasure,' Judge Dee said. 'What a nice name! Now where is your father?'

'I don't know, sir!' the boy cried out unhappily. 'When father came home, he had such a big quarrel with mother. Mother didn't have any food ready, she said there weren't even any noodles in the house. Then . . . then father began to scold her, he shouted that she had passed the afternoon with Mr Shen, the old pawn-broker. Mother started to cry, and I ran out. I thought I could perhaps borrow a package of noodles from the grocer, to make father happy again. But there was such a crowd at the grocer's that I could not get through, and I went back. But then father and mother were not there anymore, there was all that blood, all over the floor. I slipped, and I . . .'

He burst out in sobs that shook his small back. The judge drew the boy closer to him in the fold of his fur coat. They rode on in silence.

When Judge Dee saw the large gate of the Temple of Confucius looming ahead against the winter sky, he descended from his horse. Putting the boy down too, he said to the headman, 'We are nearly there. We shall leave our horses here at the gate. We'd better not give warning that we have come.'

They entered a narrow alley, lined on both sides by a row of ramshackle wooden houses. The boy pointed at a street door that stood ajar. A dim light shone behind the paper window, but the second floor was brightly lit and a confused noise of singing and shouting came from there.

'Who lives above?' Judge Dee asked, pausing in front of the door.

'That's Tailor Liu,' the boy said. 'They are having some friends in for the feast tonight.'

'You show the headman the way up there, Hsiao-pao,' the judge said. To the headman he added in a low voice: 'Leave the boy with the people upstairs, but bring that fellow Liu down here for questioning.'

Then he entered the house, followed by his two constables.

The cold, bare room was lit only by a spluttering oil lamp on a rickety corner stand. In the centre, on a large, coarsely made table, stood three bowls of cracked earthenware, and a large kitchen chopper lay at one end, spattered with blood. On the stone-flagged floor there was more blood, in a large pool.

Pointing at the chopper, the elder constable remarked, 'Someone neatly cut someone's throat with that, sir!'

Judge Dee nodded. He felt the bloodstain on the chopper with his forefinger and found that it was still wet. Looking round, he quickly surveyed the rest of the dim room. Against the back wall stood a large couch with faded blue curtains, and a small un-curtained bed was placed against the wall on the left, evidently the boy's. The plaster walls were bare, and had here and there been clumsily patched. Judge Dee went to the closed door by the side of the bedstead. It led into a small kitchen. The ashes in the stove were cold.

When the judge stepped back into the room the younger constable remarked with a sneer, 'Not a place for robbers to visit, Your Honour! I have heard about that pedlar Wang, he is as poor as a rat!'

'The motive was passion,' the judge said curtly. He pointed at a silk handkerchief that was lying on the floor, near the bed. The flickering light of the oil lamp shone on the large character 'Shen' embroidered on it in gold thread. 'After the boy had left to borrow the noodles,' Judge Dee went on, 'the pedlar found the handkerchief, left by his wife's paramour. Heated as he was by the quarrel, it was too much for him. He took the chopper and killed her. The old, old story.' He shrugged his shoulders. 'He must have gone to hide her body. Is the pedlar a strong fellow?'

'Strong as an ox, Your Honour!' the elder constable replied. 'I have often seen him about, he walks the street from morning till night carrying that heavy box on his back.'

Judge Dee glanced at the large square box covered with oil cloth standing next to the door. He nodded slowly.

The headman came in, pushing in front of him a tall, lean man. He seemed very drunk. Tottering on his feet, he gave the judge a bleary look from his small, shifty eyes. The headman grabbed his collar and forced him down on his knees. Judge Dee folded his arms in his wide sleeves and said curtly, 'A murder was committed here. State exactly what you heard and saw!'

'It must have been that woman's fault!' the tailor muttered with a thick tongue. 'Always gadding about, but not even looking at a fine upstanding fellow like me!' He hiccoughed. 'I am too poor for her, just like her husband! It's the money of the pawn-broker she's after, the slut!'

'Keep a civil tongue in your mouth!' Judge Dee ordered angrily. 'And answer my question! The ceiling here consists only of thin boards; you must have heard them quarrel!'

The headman gave him a kick in the ribs, and barked: 'Speak up!'

'I didn't hear a thing, Your Excellency!' the frightened tailor whined. 'Those bastards upstairs are all drunk, they are shouting and singing all the time! And that stupid woman of mine over-turned the bowl, and she was too drunk to wipe the stuff up. I had to shake her quite some time before I could make her set to work.'

'Nobody left the room?' Judge Dee asked.

'Not them!' the tailor muttered. 'They are all too busy gloat-ing over the pig Butcher Li slaughtered for us! And who has to do the roasting? I do! Those fellows only swill my wine, they are too lazy even to keep the coal fire burning right! The room got full of smoke, I had to open the window. Then I saw that slut run off!'

Judge Dee raised his eyebrows. He thought for a while, then asked: 'Was her husband with her?'

'Would she want him?' the tailor sneered. 'She does better alone!'

The judge quickly turned round. He stooped and scrutinized the floor. He noticed among the confused, bloody footprints those

167

of small pointed shoes leading to the door. He asked the tailor in a tense voice: 'What direction did she go?'

'To the watergate!' the man answered sullenly.

Judge Dee pulled his fur coat round him. 'Take that rascal upstairs!' he ordered the constables. Going to the door, he whispered hurriedly to the headman, 'You wait for me inside here. When Wang returns, arrest him! The pawnbroker must have looked in here to get his handkerchief just when Wang, quarrelling with his wife, discovered it. Wang killed him, and his wife fled.'

The judge went out and tramped through the snow to the next street. He mounted his horse and rode to the watergate as fast as he could. One death was enough, he reflected.

Arriving at the bottom of the stone steps leading up the gate tower, he jumped down and went hurriedly to the steep stairs, slippery with the frozen snow. On top of the tower he saw a woman, standing on the farthest parapet. She had gathered her robe round her, and with bent body looked down at the water of the city moat far below.

Judge Dee ran up to her, and laid his hand on her arm. 'You shouldn't do that, Mrs Wang!' he said gravely. 'Killing yourself won't bring the dead back to life!'

The woman shrank back against the battlement and looked at the judge with startled eyes, her lips parted in fright. He saw that although her face was drawn and haggard, she was still handsome in a common sort of way.

'You must be from the tribunal!' she faltered. 'That means they have discovered that my poor husband murdered him! And it's all my fault!' She burst out in heart-breaking sobs.

'Was it the pawnbroker Shen he murdered?' Judge Dee asked.

She nodded her head forlornly. Then she cried out: 'I am such a fool! I swear there was nothing between Shen and me; I only wanted to tease my husband a little. . . .' She pushed a wet lock back from her forehead. 'Shen had ordered a set of embroidered handkerchiefs from me, to give to his concubine as a New Year's present. I had not told my husband, I wanted to surprise him with the money. Tonight, when Wang found the last handkerchief I was working on, he went to get the kitchen knife, shouting that he would kill Shen and me. I fled outside; I tried to get to my sister in the next street, but the house was closed. And when I came back to our place, my husband was gone and . . . there was all that blood.' She covered her face with her hands, then added sobbing: 'Shen . . . he must have come for the handkerchief and . . . Wang killed him. It's all my fault, how can I go on living when my husband . . . ?'

'Remember that you have your son to look after,' Judge Dee interrupted her. He gripped her arm firmly and led her to the stairs.

Back at the house he told the headman to take the woman upstairs. When the headman had done so, the judge said, 'We shall stand close to the door, against the wall. We have only to wait for the murderer's return. Wang killed Shen here, then went out to hide his victim's body. He planned to come back here to clean up that blood, but his son brought us here, and his plan has fallen through.' After a while he added with a sigh, 'I am sorry for that boy, he's a likable little fellow!'

The four men stood against the wall, two on either side of the door, Judge Dee next to the pedlar's box. Upstairs, some coarse voices were shouting in argument.

Suddenly the door opened and a big, broad-shouldered man came in. The constables jumped on him. Taken by surprise, before he knew what was happening they had chained Wang's arms behind his back, and pressed him down on his knees. A package wrapped in oil paper fell from his sleeve, noodles spilled on the floor. One of the constables kicked the package into a corner.

Upstairs some people were dancing. The thin boards of the ceiling bent and creaked.

'Don't throw away good food!' Judge Dee barked, irritated at the constable. 'Pick that up!'

Thus rebuked, the constable made haste to scoop up the noodles. When placing them on the table, he muttered, 'They aren't much good any more, the dirt that came down from the ceiling has spoiled them.'

'The rascal has blood on his right hand, Your Honour!' the

169

headman who had been inspecting Wang's chains exclaimed excitedly.

Wang had been staring with wide eyes at the blood on the floor in front of him. His lips were moving but no sound came. Now he lifted his face up to the judge and brought out: 'Where is my wife? What has happened to her?'

Judge Dee sat down on the box and folded his hands in his wide sleeves. He said coldly: 'It is I, the magistrate, who asks questions here! Tell me . . .'

'Where is my wife?' Wang shouted frantically. He wanted to scramble up but the headman hit him over the head with the heavy handle of his whip. Wang dazedly shook his head, and stammered: 'My wife . . . and my son . . .'

'Speak up! What happened here tonight?' the judge asked.

'Tonight . . .' Wang said in a toneless voice, then hesitated.

The headman gave him a kick. 'Answer and speak the truth!' he growled.

Wang frowned. He again looked at the blood on the floor. At last he began, 'Tonight, when I was walking home, the grocer told me that the pawnbroker Shen had been here. And when I came in, there was nothing to eat, not even our New Year's noodles. I told my wife I did not want her any more, that she could go to that fellow Shen, and stay there. I said that the entire neighbourhood knew that he visited her when I was out. She would not say yes or no. Then I found that handkerchief there by the bed. I went for the chopper. I would first kill her and then go and finish off that fellow Shen. But when I came back from the kitchen with the chopper, my wife had run away. I grabbed the handkerchief, I wanted to throw that in Shen's face before I cut his throat. But I scratched my hand on the needle stuck in it.'

Wang paused. He bit his lips and swallowed. 'I knew then what an utter fool I had been. Shen had not dropped the handkerchief there; it was one he had ordered from her, and on which she was still working. . . . I went out to look for my wife. I went to her sister's home, but nobody was there. Then I walked to Shen's shop; I wanted to pawn my jacket and buy something nice for my wife. But Shen said he owed me a string of coppers for a set of twenty handkerchiefs he had ordered from her. The last one had not been quite finished when he had looked in at our house in the afternoon, but his concubine had been very pleased with the ones he had given her. And since it was New Year's eve, he said, he would pay me anyway. I bought a package of noodles, and a paper flower for my wife, and came here.' Gazing at the judge, he burst out: 'Tell me, what has happened to her? Where is she?'

The headman guffawed. He shouted: 'What a string of stupid lies the dog is telling! The bastard hopes to gain time!' Lifting the handle of his whip, he asked the judge: 'Shall I knock his teeth in, Your Honour, to make the truth come out a bit easier?'

Judge Dee shook his head. Slowly stroking his long sidewhiskers, he looked fixedly at the drawn face of the pedlar kneeling before him. Then he ordered the headman: 'See whether he has a paper flower on him!'

The headman put his hand in the pedlar's bosom, and brought out a red paper flower. He held it up for the judge to see, then threw it disdainfully on the floor and put his foot on it.

Judge Dee rose. He walked over to the bedstead, picked up the handkerchief and looked it over carefully. Then he went to the table and stood there for a while, staring down at the dirty noodles on the piece of oil paper. The only sound heard was the heavy breathing of the kneeling man.

Suddenly the uproar of voices on the floor above burst out again. Judge Dee looked up at the ceiling. Then he turned to the headman and ordered: 'Bring those two down here!'

As soon as the pedlar saw his wife and his son, his mouth opened in astonished delight. He cried out: 'Heaven be praised, you are safe!' He would have jumped up, but the constables roughly pressed him down again.

His wife threw herself down on the floor in front of the kneeling man. She moaned, 'Forgive me, forgive me! I was such a fool, I only wanted to tease you! What have I done, what have I done! Now you have . . . They will take you away and . . .'

'Rise, you two!' the stern voice of the judge interrupted her. At his peremptory gesture the two constables let go of Wang's shoulders.

'Take the chains off him!' Judge Dee ordered. As the dumb-

171

AS SOON AS THE PEDLAR SAW HIS WIFE AND SON . . .

founded headman carried out this order, the judge continued to Wang, 'Tonight your foolish jealousy nearly made you lose your wife. It is your son who averted a terrible tragedy, he came to warn me just in time. Let tonight be a lesson to you—to both of you, man and wife. New Year's eve is a time to remember. To remember the blessings Heaven has bestowed on you, the gifts we are wont to take too much for granted and forget too soon. You love each other, you are in good health, and you have a fine son. That is more than many can say! Make the resolution that henceforward you shall try to prove yourselves worthy of those blessings!' Turning to the small boy, he patted him on his head and added: 'Lest you forget, I order you to change this boy's name into Ta-pao. That means "Big Treasure"!'

He signalled to his three men and went to the door.

'But . . . Your Honour, that murder . . .' the woman faltered.

Pausing in the open doorway, the judge said with a bleak smile: 'There was no murder. When the people upstairs had killed a pig, the tailor's wife overturned the bowl in which they had poured the blood, and she was too drunk to wipe it up at once. It leaked through the cracks in the ceiling on to the table and the floor in this room. Good-bye!'

The woman put her hand over her mouth to suppress a cry of joy. Her husband smiled a little foolishly at her, then stooped and picked up the paper flower. Having clumsily smoothed out its petals, he stepped up to her, and stuck the flower in her hair. The boy looked up at his parents, a broad smile on his small round face.

The headman had led Judge Dee's horse in front of the door. Only after the judge had jumped into the saddle did he suddenly realize that his rheumatism was gone.

The gong of the nightwatch announced midnight. Firecrackers started an uproar in the market place. As the judge urged on his horse he turned round in his saddle and called out:

'Happy New Year!'

He doubted whether the three people in the doorway had heard him. It didn't really matter.

COLOPHON

JUDGE DEE was a historical person. His full name was Dee Jen-djieh and he lived from A.D. 630 to 700. In the latter half of his career he became a Minister of State, and through his wise counsels exercised a beneficial influence on the internal and external affairs of the T'ang empire.

However, it is chiefly because of his reputation as a detector of crimes, acquired while serving as district magistrate, that his name lives on among the Chinese people. Today the Chinese still consider him their master-detective, and his name is as popular with them as that of Sherlock Holmes with us.

Although the stories told in the present volume are entirely fictional, I utilized some data from old Chinese crime literature, especially a thirteenth-century manual of jurisprudence and detection which I published ten years ago in an English translation (T'ang-yin-pi-shih, Sinica Leidensia vol. X, E. J. Brill, Leiden 1956). The final passage of 'The Murder on the Lotus Pond' was suggested by Cases 33A and B recorded in that book, and the weighing of the sarcophagus described in 'The Coffins of the Emperor' by a note added to Case 35B.

The design of the incense-clock utilized in 'Five Auspicious Clouds' I copied from the Hsiang-yin-t'u-k'ao, a collection of such patterns published in 1878; I used the same source for the pattern of the maze in The Chinese Maze Murders.

Note that in China the surname precedes the personal name. Also that in Judge Dee's time the Chinese wore no pig-tails; that custom was imposed upon them in A.D. 1644 by the Manchu conquerors. Men did their long hair up in a top-knot, they wore caps both inside and outside the house. They didn't smoke, tobacco and opium were introduced into China only many centuries later.

Tokyo: 1967   Robert van Gulik

JUDGE DEE CHRONOLOGY

(Fictitious, except for his birthdate, and the historical note at the end)
covering 15 novels and 8 short stories.

Time, place and Judge Dee's office	Titles (the short stories of the present volume are marked by an asterisk)	Information on Judge Dee, his family, his lieutenants, and persons who appear in more than one story (page numbers refer to the first London editions)
A.D. 630 Tai-yuan, capital of Shansi Province.		Judge Dee born. Receives elementary education at home. Passes the provincial literary examinations.
650 The capital.		Judge Dee's father appointed Imperial Councillor in the capital. Judge Dee acts as his father's private secretary, marries his First and Second Ladies. Passes metropolitan literary examination, and is appointed secretary in the Imperial Archives.
663 Magistrate of Peng-lai, a district on the northeast coast of the Chinese Empire.	*The Chinese Gold Murders* (London 1959). The Murdered Magistrate, The Bolting Bride, The Butchered Bully.	Judge Dee's first independent official post. Proceeds there accompanied by Sergeant Hoong. Meets on the way Ma Joong and Chiao Tai. First mention of the sword Rain Dragon; Chiao Tai foresees he will be killed by that sword (p. 31). Ch. XV describes adventures of Miss Tsao.
	*Five Auspicious Clouds	One week after Judge Dee's arrival in Peng-lai. Mrs Ho: suicide or murder? Solved by Judge Dee alone.
	*The Red Tape Murder	One month later. A military murder, solved by Judge Dee, assisted by Ma Joong and Chiao Tai. Colonel Meng appears.
	*He Came with the Rain	Six months later. Murder of a pawnbroker, solved by Judge Dee alone. Colonel Meng is again referred to. Judge Dee decides to marry Miss Tsao as his Third Lady.

JUDGE DEE CHRONOLOGY (cont.)

Time, place and Judge Dee's office	Titles (the short stories of the present volume are marked by an asterisk)	Information on Judge Dee, his family, his lieutenants, and persons who appear in more than one story (page numbers refer to the first London editions)
663	*The Lacquer Screen* (London 1962). The Lacquer Screen, The Credulous Merchant, The Faked Accounts.	Solved by Judge Dee, assisted by Chiao Tai, during a brief sojourn in the district Wei-ping. Second reference to Chiao Tai dying by the sword (p. 140).
666 Magistrate of Han-yuan, a district on the bank of a lake, near the capital.	*The Chinese Lake Murders* (London 1960). The Drowned Courtesan, The Vanished Bride, The Spendthrift Councillor.	Solved by Judge Dee, Hoong, Ma Joong and Chiao Tai. His future fourth lieutenant Tao Gan here makes his first appearance (p. 153). The rich landowner Han Yung-han appears (passim). Description of the King of the Beggars of Han-yuan (p. 118).
	The Morning of the Monkey (in The Monkey and the Tiger [London 1965]).	Murder of a tramp, solved by Judge Dee and Tao Gan; Tao Gan is definitively taken into Judge Dee's service. The King of the Beggars reappears (p. 31). Han Yung-han mentioned (p. 59).
	The Haunted Monastery (London 1961). The Embalmed Abbot, The Pious Maid, The Morose Monk.	Scene is laid in an old Taoist temple, in the mountains of Han-yuan. Murders solved by Judge Dee, with Tao Gan. Judge Dee's attitude to his wives described on p. 12.
	*The Murder on the Lotus Pond	The murder of an old poet, solved by Judge Dee, with Ma Joong.
668 Magistrate of Poo-yang, a large, flourishing district in Kiangsu Province, on the Grand Canal.	*The Chinese Bell Murders* (London 1958). The Rape Murder in Half Moon Street, The Secret of the Buddhist Temple, The Mysterious Skeleton.	Solved by Judge Dee, with his four lieutenants Sergeant Hoong, Ma Joong, Chiao Tai and Tao Gan. Introduction of Sheng Pa, Head of the Beggars (passim). Introduction of Magistrate Lo, of the neighbouring district (Ch. IX).

JUDGE DEE CHRONOLOGY (cont.)

Time, place and Judge Dee's office	Titles (the short stories of the present volume are marked by an asterisk)	Information on Judge Dee, his family, his lieutenants, and persons who appear in more than one story (page numbers refer to the first London editions)
676 Magistrate of Pei-chow, a desolate district up in the barren north.	The Chinese Nail Murders (London 1961), The Headless Corpse, The Paper Cat, The Murdered Merchant.	After only a few months in this new post, Judge Dee was appointed Lord Chief Justice, in the capital. In Pei-chow he solves several particularly cruel murders, with Hoong, Ma Joong, Chiao Tai and Tao Gan; but Sergeant Hoong is killed while working on a case. The antecedents of Judge Dee's three wives are given on p. 116. Introduction of Mrs Kuo, the Lady of the Medicine Hill (p. 38).
	The Night of the Tiger (In The Monkey and the Tiger [London 1965]).	Murder of a young girl solved by Judge Dee alone when, on his way from Pei-chow to the capital, he has to stay overnight in a lonely country house. References to Mrs Kuo and Sergeant Hoong's death, on p. 91.
677 Lord Chief Justice, in the imperial capital.	The Willow Pattern (London 1965), The Willow Pattern, The Steep Staircase, The Murdered Bondmaid.	Judge Dee has taken up his new office of Lord Chief Justice, Ma Joong and Chiao Tai have been appointed Colonels of the Guard, Tao Gan chief secretary of the Metropolitan Court. Ma Joong marries the Yuan twin sisters.
681 Lord Chief Justice.	Murder in Canton (London 1966), The Vanished Censor, The Smaragdine Dancer, The Golden Bell.	Scene is laid in Canton, where Judge Dee has been sent on a special mission. Murders solved by Judge Dee, with the assistance of Chiao Tai and Tao Gan. Chiao Tai is killed by the sword Rain Dragon, Tao Gan decides to marry Miss Liang. Reference to Mrs Kuo and the tragedy on Medicine Hill on p. 160.

Historical Note. Judge Dee died in A.D. 700, at the age of seventy. He was survived by two sons, Dee Guang-se and Dee Djing-hui, who had an honourable official career without, however, particularly distinguishing themselves. It was his grandson Dee Djien-mo who inherited his grandfather's remarkable personality and great wisdom; he died as governor of the Imperial Capital.